GW00599368

The Sign in the Moonlight
AND OTHER STORIES

Also by David Tallerman

The Tales of Easie Damasco:

Giant Thief (2012)
Crown Thief (2012)
Prince Thief (2013)

Patchwerk (2016)

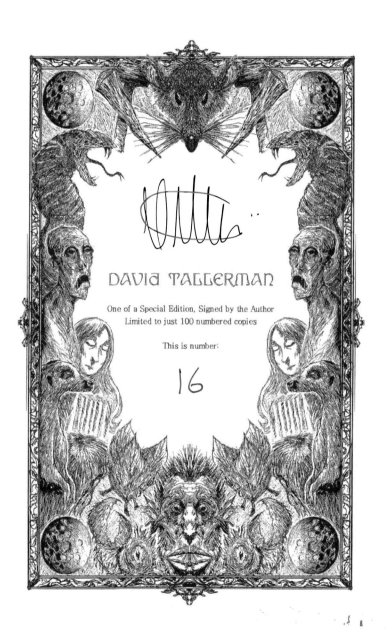

DAVID TALLERMAN

One of a Special Edition, Signed by the Author
Limited to just 100 numbered copies

This is number:

16

The Sign in the Moonlight

AND OTHER STORIES

David Tallerman

Illustrations by Duncan Kay

NewCon Press
England

First hardback edition, published in the UK 2016 by
NewCon Press
41, Wheatsheaf Road,
Alconbury Weston,
Cambs,
PE28 4LF

NCP97 Hardback
10 9 8 7 6 5 4 3 2 1

ISBN: 978-1-910935-15-6 (hardback)
Cover art and internal illustrations by Duncan Kay
Editorial meddling by Ian Whates
Interior layout by Storm Constantine

Author's Dedication:

For Rafe, who read so many of these stories before anyone else did, and who helped make so many of them what they are now.

Thanks for being around from the start.

– David

Artist's Dedication:

For Mum.

– Duncan

Contents

Introduction

Adrian Tchaikovsky

I first heard the name Tallerman when his publisher tapped me to give a quote for his new fantasy novel *Giant Thief*. This was at a time when the vast majority of new fantasy coming out was of a decidedly low-fantasy, high-grimdark nature. The title alone caught my attention. Giants? As in actual giants? Was the thief a giant? Did the thief steal giants? Or was the title simply an indication of the enormous scale of larceny being perpetrated? In retrospect, something of all of them, especially as the series went on (with *Crown Thief* and *Prince Thief*). The adventures of Easie Damasco were something of a breath of fresh air in the genre right then: a hero who actually got out into the great outdoors rather than moping about in the slums; a thief who, rather than concentrating on being the most daring or the most skilled or the grimmest, would settle for being the most still-alive at the end of the story (and, if possible, the richest, but that never seems to come off for poor Easie.)

Moving closer to the task in hand, though, David is also a consummate writer of short fiction. His writing is a common sight in a wide variety of genre magazines and websites: *Interzone*, *Clarkesworld*, *Beneath Ceaseless Skies*, *Nightmare*, *Lightspeed* and many others. Varied, also, are the anthologies that have hosted David's work – a full bibliography can be found on his site davidtallerman.co.uk but he has been picked up by a wide range of presses.

So what has David got in store for us within these pages? A more traumatic journey than one of Easie

9

Damasco's; a trip into the darker side of his imagination. There will be ghosts and monsters, and more alien entities lurking in the shadows. Every story here opens a door onto some human trauma: loss, grief, death, murder and madness, encounters with the horrors of the supernatural, and perhaps the worse horrors that the simple mundane world can inflict. The otherworld calls to a young girl through a door in an ancient barrow; a prisoner shares his cell with a thing he only knows he cannot look at; explorers follow ill-shadowed rumours into inhospitable lands, to find themselves stepping away from everything they ever knew. A lot of David's writing straddles and blurs the line between the natural and supernatural. There are many hauntings in these tales, and whilst some are traditional spectres, the stories collected here show how people can be haunted by far more than spirits. Guilt, fear and post-traumatic shock are all equally as effective at riding the shoulders of these protagonists: it's always so much harder to escape from the ghosts within.

You'll find some Lovecraftian influences here – and the best kind, where nobody ever mentions Great Cthulhu or starts conjuring with all those hard-to-pronounce names. There's definitely a sniff of M. R. James, too, and perhaps a little Arthur Machen: the footsteps in which most writers of the speculative and the unnerving walk for a time. There is a definite timelessness, too. David has a very deft hand for conjuring past ages, both in the details of the stories and the style he presents them in – there are stories here that could come straight out of the pulp journals of the 30s, others that have the mannered feel of Victoriana, and others again with more modern sensibilities and humour, but all are presented with the intensity and focus that characterises David's short fiction.

Some of the stories presented here are reprints of tales that are otherwise hard to find, others are original to this collection. All of them are thought-provoking and finely crafted, and none outstay their welcome. I hope you enjoy them as much as I have.

Adrian Tchaikovsky
2016

The Burning Room

I can't say for sure what drew me to that ill-fated attic room. It was cheap, which was crucial, and I much preferred a landlady to a landlord, even if her behaviour was curious. These concerns were very real. Looking back, though, I wonder if they were decisive.

There's no doubt that my circumstances were difficult. I'd moved for the promise of employment with a small millinery firm, and to lodge with a kind-hearted aunt. The job had materialised, though with a lower wage than promised. The aunt, however, had fallen sick a week before, and died in hospital a day after my arrival. I'd found myself wandering the poorer parts of London, desperate for a residence that my meagre income would support.

Thus, for all her strangeness, Mrs Faraday seemed a blessing. She interviewed me in a small, drab kitchen, claustrophobically gloomy with the heavy curtains drawn. There were indications of poverty, but signs of former comfort also: the tablecloth, though faded, had once been fine; the chipped crockery in the cabinet was china of a more expensive sort.

"I wouldn't let it," she said, "if I weren't very desperate. I've put off doing so these past years since I lost my Daniel, Lord knows I have. But times are hard."

So she was widowed. That explained the odd mixture of penury and luxury. "I'll be quiet, and no bother," I replied.

She stared at me. I couldn't have hazarded a guess at her age. Her hair was grey, her eyes seemed washed of vitality, but her skin was unlined and seemed to belong to a much younger woman. She ran her fingertips down the swath of crimson scarring that spread from her cheek to beyond her collarbone, and said, "Miss Taversham, it isn't myself I'm worried for. Do you sleep deeply?"

"I imagine so. It isn't something I've considered."

"Then probably you do. Will you see the room?"

"I'd like to."

From the kitchen, Mrs Faraday led me up a narrow staircase pressed into the side of the house. At the first floor was a small landing with two exits, which we continued past. My initial view of the second floor was a corridor with a single door half way along its length. I could see from the curve of the ceiling that we were in the roof. Mrs Faraday led me to the door, opened it with a key, and ushered me through. Once I had entered, she left me, saying, "I'll wait downstairs."

I watched her retreating back in perplexity. Only when she was out of view did I think to examine the room that might be my new home. I was surprised by how spacious it was: it ran the full breadth of the house, and though the arch above constricted the distance there was a portion of wall all around that reached to about waist height.

This was more than large enough for my needs, and adequately furnished. To my left stood a single bed with a nightstand. Opposite was an elderly mahogany wardrobe, and to my right a washstand, a set of drawers, and a chair. A single sash window opened in that direction, giving a view over the rooftops, their red tile a dour brown in the autumn light.

The whole was simple, even plain, and yet it struck a chord with me. I imagined myself sat at the window, reading verse under the bloody light of a London sunset, and a tingle ran up my spine. There was an atmosphere to the room, something not far removed from the gothic romances I'd delighted in as a girl – a sense of melancholy, and of something deeper still.

If a first glance had convinced me to take it, a more rational voice warned me not to be overhasty. I passed five minutes in careful investigation, but turned up nothing, for little could be hidden in such an empty room. Then, as I turned to leave, I happened to glance at the ceiling, where the roof beams half-protruded through the plaster. They were painted white, but at the spot I'd noticed the paint had peeled, revealing the wood beneath. It was black, and when I pressed with my finger, it crumbled.

Someone had evidently decorated to disguise fire damage. That suggested answers to some of my questions regarding Mrs Faraday and her odd behaviour. Surely, here was the source of that horrible scar I'd noticed earlier. Perhaps she was hesitant to let the room because something unpleasant had occurred there, or because she doubted its safety.

My one concern had been that my prospective landlady suffered from some nervous illness, which might make her company difficult. Strangely, that fear relaxed with this hint of an explanation.

Letting myself out, I noticed the key was still in the door, so I locked it as I left. I made my way carefully down the two steep flights of stairs. Mrs Faraday had made tea, and when I came in she was sitting staring at the pot. She started when I coughed, and looked at me almost in fright. Finally, she asked, "Is it suitable?"

"It is. I'd like to take it."

"The price isn't excessive?"

In truth, the price was quite the opposite. "It's appropriate to my means."

"That's good. I'll wash and cook for you for a little extra, but you can decide on that later. When can you move in?"

"Straight away, if that's acceptable."

She sighed as she nodded, and I couldn't help but notice the shadow of emotion that flickered across her eyes.

True to her word, Mrs Faraday made dinner enough for

both of us that night, a chicken stew. She even, to my astonishment, produced a bottle of sherry afterwards. Yet, as pleasant as hot food and kind treatment were after my long travel and the shock of my aunt's death, Mrs Faraday made for awkward company. She hardly spoke and, though she answered any questions I put, my imagination was soon exhausted. It was before nine when I made my excuses and retired.

Autumn was proving to be bitter. Mrs Faraday had left a fire burning in the small hearth, and I added more wood, but it made little difference. I washed quickly, hurried into my nightgown and climbed into my new bed. With the quilt wrapped tight around me, I found I was somewhat warmer. I snuffed the candle on the nightstand and settled down to sleep.

Whether because of excitement at my new circumstances or sorrow at the week's unexpected tragedy, sleep didn't come readily. I despaired of trying after a while, and opened my eyes. A little moonlight had strayed around the edges of the curtains, daubing the room in shades of grey that edged to blackness in the corners and around the furnishings. I noticed details that had escaped me earlier: cobwebs mazelike between the rafters, and what seemed to be dark stains on the floorboards. The fire had burned down, and the room was very cold.

As I lay staring, that began to change. It was so subtle at first that I hardly noticed. Then it occurred to me that my arms, which I'd unconsciously placed outside the bedclothes, were prickled with sweat. I glanced again at the hearth but saw nothing except a hint of dying embers. Now I could feel heat on my face, and my hair stuck in moist curls. I wondered if I might be ill.

Without warning, the cold returned – worse now, so that I was sure it must be below freezing. I dragged the quilt around myself, but that hardly stopped me shivering. The room seemed darker than before, the stray shapes of moonlight sharper but less real.

Behind me, the door slammed, and I nearly fell from the bed. I twisted round, only to find that there was nothing to see. The door was closed. Could the sound have come from a neighbouring house? I was certain it hadn't.

It occurred to me then that there *was* something before the door, resembling the faintest glow of phosphor, about half way up its surface. Slowly it spread, upward at first and then downwards as well. Soon I could recognise something resembling a figure in outline, pale and insubstantial. I realised I'd stopped shaking, though I was terribly afraid. I don't believe anything could have made me tear my eyes away.

The figure moved suddenly, with long strides that carried him the length of the room. He passed quite close to me. I could see the curtains through him, but they seemed flimsy and unconvincing, as if formed from greased paper, and the figure more real in comparison. I thought I read a hint of features, an aquiline nose and intent eyes. Then he had passed me. He stopped close to the wall, made a curious shrugging motion, reached out with one arm, and was gone.

You may imagine how well I slept through the remainder of the night. However, it was only at first that fear kept me awake. Soon anxiety gave way to curiosity. I was quick to realise I hadn't been harmed, or even directly disturbed by the phantom. More, I was aware that I'd witnessed something mysterious, not only as a spiritual quandary but also on a practical level: what was the explanation for my visitor's route across the chamber, and his action on reaching the far wall? These questions, and an exciting sense of eeriness, held sleep at bay.

I must have drifted off at some point, though, for I awoke late the next day. I decided immediately that I'd say nothing to Mrs Faraday unless she asked directly, and though she looked at me inquisitively when I went down for breakfast, she said nothing. It seemed likely from her veiled warnings that she had some connection with the spirit, and I didn't want to upset her. I'd never find another room so suited to my circumstances. If my co-tenant were not completely intolerable, I'd have to stay.

I spent the day familiarising myself with the neighbourhood and my route to work, whilst mulling over the events of the previous night. They seemed fragmentary and unlikely beneath the chill autumn daylight. I probed my own mental state for any trace of hysteria, and felt my brow to see if I was running a temperature. No, as far as the tests were valid, I seemed sound. I'd seen what I'd seen. I couldn't doubt it.

So what did it mean? Through the course of the day, and then as I shared an evening meal with Mrs Faraday, I could hazard no answer. It was only when I'd returned to my room, and purely by accident, that a clue was revealed. I'd been for another short walk after tea, prior to retiring. As I stood before the wardrobe with arm outstretched, about to hang my overcoat, a shudder ran through me.

In that moment I'd imagined my posture as another would see it. The thrill had been one of recognition.

The pose was the same, but the position was different. For the scene to correlate, the wardrobe would have to be half a dozen feet further towards the window. In a moment of inspiration, I emptied the contents and set about moving it. Though the closet was of solid, heavy wood, I succeeded in levering it, by a process of short turns, to where the spirit had perceived it – and where gouges in the floorboards implied it had once stood.

Pleased with myself, I settled into bed. My first thought was to wait in the hope of seeing the apparition, but common sense reminded me that tomorrow I started a new employment. Instead, I tried to sleep and, after the deprivation of the previous night, met with quick success.

When I woke, it was to a sense of ferocious heat on my

neck and face. I had no idea of the time, except that it was still dark. The temperature was so unpleasant that I wondered if there wasn't a fire. However, as soon as the thought had crossed my mind, it went, to be replaced by the appalling cold I'd experienced the night before. I looked automatically towards the door.

This time there was no sound. Instead, the door appeared to flicker, as though for an instant it was open and closed at the same time. This time, too, the figure materialised more quickly, dispersing out of nothing so abruptly that I started in alarm. He seemed clearer, now, more fully formed.

I hadn't expected to be afraid, yet I was.

He passed by me again, and I could see how intent his expression was. I even gathered some impression of his clothes, which were informal and very outmoded. He didn't look at me. When he reached the far end, he didn't fade as before, and I could see clearly how he removed a coat and hung it on the peg there, just as I'd imagined.

I was glad when he didn't dematerialise, scared though I was. Instead, he paced rapidly towards the window and stopped before the washstand. His back was to me, but I heard the splash of water. Then he stepped to the left and stared intently at the wall.

For an instant, to my horror, another phantom face seemed to gaze back from thin air. Yet the figure didn't appear concerned, and before I could be certain he turned towards me. He crossed the room, to a space six feet from the end of my bed, and knelt down – at which point he disappeared, taking that awful cold with him.

My new employment proved physically wearisome but mentally undemanding. I found I had plenty of intellectual energy left to muse over the strange drama that had enlivened my night.

I was certain my visitor wanted something from me.

His unquiet made him repeat a set of behaviours that required a witness, or perhaps an interpreter. He entered the room, took off his coat, and washed his hands. All those were actions that anyone might perform on returning home. Then what? At the last, he'd appeared to be kneeling. To open a drawer, to pray, or to converse with someone who was sitting down, perhaps? What of that horrible moment in between, when he'd gazed into nothingness and some other had stared back from the void?

I was left alone that night and the following. I was glad of the undisturbed sleep, since my work had left me exhausted, but each morning I woke frustrated by an enigma left half-solved. Then – it was Wednesday evening, and I was walking home through densely thronged streets, beneath a drizzling sky of packed cloud – I happened to glance at a dress in a shop window. I was alarmed by another face staring back, until I recognised it as my own reflection.

Then realisation hit me like a blow.

The rest of the week passed without activity, and I willed the days away impatiently. Finally, Saturday came. I'd received my first pay on Friday evening, and after settling my rent with Mrs Faraday I still had a few coins left. I spent most of Saturday scouring flea markets and the dingier sort of antique shops. Eventually I found something suitable within my modest means: a full-length mirror tall enough for a man to view himself in.

That night I put the mirror in its place beside the washstand. Then, abruptly inspired, I moved my bed until it lay before where the spirit had appeared to be kneeling.

I couldn't think of sleeping. Though I went to bed, I left my candle burning and sat reading with pillows heaped behind me. I was determined: I was a lavish host, and I deserved a grateful visitor. Yet at first there was no sound except the wind shrugging the branches in the public gardens and rattling the chimney pots, and nothing to see but words crawling beneath my eyes. Presently I found myself sleepy and my eyelids sagging.

The candle dimmed, or seemed to, until – though it still burned with a pale, elongated flame – the room was as dark as if it were unlit. Again, there was the sense of heat crawling over me, as though sickness raged under my skin. Sweat coursed down my face. I felt certain I'd panic, and dropped my book to the floor.

Then the cold came. The sweat turned to ice-like droplets on my skin. I looked towards the door, at once entranced and hardly daring to look.

For a long while there was nothing to see but blackness on blackness, though the cold didn't retreat one iota. The slam of the door made me start backward, the more so because I could see the door itself hadn't moved. Suddenly he was there, a luminous silhouette poised in the dark. I drew away instinctively, dragging the quilt into a barricade around me. Still, I couldn't help staring as he crossed the room, shrugged off his long coat, and hung it upon the closet.

As before, he continued to the washstand and scrubbed half-visible hands. Then he stepped to gaze into the mirror, where his reflection was now layered upon the cracked glass rather than hanging in the ether. Satisfied by whatever he saw there, he turned away and strode rapidly towards me. I could see his face clearly.

What I saw there horrified me.

I tried to push further back, but the wall blocked my retreat, and all I could do was watch his approach. There was something appalling in his deliberateness. Reaching the edge of the bed, he knelt, bringing his face very close to mine. I'd never imagined such fury, such hatred.

"Unfaithful. Untrue." The words were harsh and faint, like the rattle of a distant train.

"No." He wasn't talking to me, of course. Still, I felt

sure he was wrong.

"You've sinned against me, wife." His voice was stronger now – though not as strong as the hands caught suddenly about my throat. I knew they weren't real. When I tried to resist, my own limbs passed through his without hindrance. Yet my throat constricted. My lungs burned, craving air. I fought harder, flailed at and through his contorted face.

To my shock, a blow made contact – or more likely, the woman whose part I played had struck in that same instant. He recoiled, lips curled around a snarl, three parallel lines of red drawn across his cheek. He drew his fist back to strike me. As he did so, his elbow upset the candle. I watched as it fell from the nightstand, struck the floorboards and snuffed out.

Inexplicably, other flames licked up around the fallen candle, as though it had set light to a rug or some garment. This was no normal blaze: insubstantial, it burned with a white glow brightening to pallid blue. I knew this was as phantasmal as the figure before me, that it belonged to the past tragedy I'd found myself drawn into. Still, I could feel the ferocious heat.

Finally, I abandoned myself to terror. I screamed with all my strength. Yet the spirit seemed unconcerned; he only stared, perplexed, at the conflagration licking around his boots. Then he stepped back, towards the middle of the room.

My scream had brought other attention. I could hear running footsteps below.

The spectre was pawing at the flames, which rose all about him now and lapped eagerly at his clothes. He struggled in vain against a fire as incorporeal as himself. His efforts only fanned it into new fervour.

The hurrying feet reached the head of the stair and padded along the corridor. My door flew open, and Mrs Faraday took two steps into the room. Her fingers darted to the scar upon her cheek. Her expression was almost more ghastly than the incandescent figure writhing before her.

She stopped, reached out. "Not again. Oh, not again!" Then, in barely more than a croak, she said, "It wasn't true. I only ever loved you."

She clutched one hand against her breast. I wondered what the gesture signified, until she crumpled to her knees. Her face was absolutely pale, except for the livid red of the scar. She mouthed something, though no sound came.

Diaphanous blue flames licked as high as her shoulders and crawled across her nightgown. She made one more attempt to speak, and finally found her voice: "I loved you," she repeated.

Then she fell forward and lay quite still.

My first thought was to rush to her aid, though I knew it was to no avail. What had been terrible once was insufferable a second time; her heart, long weakened, had failed entirely. Still, in a muddle of shock and horror, my instinct told me that here was a person in anguish whom I must try to help.

I'd got as far as placing bare heels on the wooden boards before I saw how he'd moved. The flames were still licking, already reaching to the ceiling, in purest blues and greens – but now he stood oblivious. All his attention was focused on the woman lying crumpled at his feet. His disregard seemed to tame the conflagration: it faded, not as any earthly fire would but by degrees of colour, growing paler and more vapid. When he stepped free to kneel beside her, it left no residue on his clothing, only continued to flicker weakly where he'd been.

He ran an ashen hand through her hair, though not one strand moved an iota. He placed a kiss on her forehead, leaving no shadow of breath. Then he threw his head back and howled a cry that was a thousand times more dreadful for its silence.

I blinked tears out of my eyes. I opened them to

darkness. Gone were the spectral flames. Gone was their unreal heat. Gone was the vestige of a man for whom realisation had come too late.

I think I hid in the kitchen for the rest of the night. I don't remember any of it very clearly. My first definite memory is of rousing a neighbour, a matronly woman who sent one of her great brood of children for a policeman.

I was certain they would blame me, somehow. Yet in the end a story was pieced together, with little intervention from myself, which found me entirely blameless. There was no question that Mrs Faraday had died of natural causes. By unfortunate chance, she'd happened to meet her end in the room of her young tenant, who of course was upset and even a touch delirious. What concern was any of this for the city's constabulary? By the time I could give the matter my full attention, it had been forgotten in the eyes of the law.

An unnamed relative paid for the meagre funeral that followed a couple of days later. Whoever they were, they felt no urge to attend. Elizabeth Faraday was buried beside her husband Daniel. I stood alone with the priest, listening to words I found hard to reconcile with what I'd seen. I couldn't help but flinch when, in closing his brief speech, he said that their souls were at last reunited.

I know now beyond doubt that there are spaces beyond death. I can't judge whether heaven or hell lie within their geography. Nor can I guess what deeds, if such realms exist, would draw a soul one way or the other, what sins might be deemed forgivable.

Nevertheless, I pray with all my heart for that sad, shattered woman to be free at last of the man who, doubting, tried to take her life, and who succeeded in the very end.

~

I'm a sucker for ghost stories, so it's probably appropriate that there are three of the things in this collection.

I also don't believe in ghosts, spirits or any sort of afterlife, which begs the question of just what the appeal is. Then again, perhaps a lack of belief is precisely the charm; just because I can't persuade myself that there's any reward or punishment waiting after death, it doesn't make the idea less intriguing. Still, I suspect there's more going on here than my indulging in morbid curiosity. Ghost stories, after all, are about a great many fascinating things: grief and loss and our fears of mortality, the intersection of past and present, and the question of what, if anything, we leave behind us when we go.

I have a theory that most ghost stories are essentially mysteries, and that's certainly true of "The Burning Room": it plays out, basically, as a detective story, with the principle difference being that the crime in question is dramatized over and over, as our protagonist finds herself confronted by the tragic history of that suspiciously cheap room she's talked herself into renting. Another impetus, as with many of these stories, was to take a traditional genre — say, the Victorian ghost tale — and try and modernize or otherwise upend it in some way I found particularly interesting. In this case, that meant giving my female protagonist more voice and leeway than she might have had in similar tales from the period. The estimable Ms. Taversham isn't one to be frightened away by things going bump in the night; instead she'd rather interpret the horror she encounters as a problem to be solved, and to be seen through to its bitter end.

Oh, and the title was meant as a reference to H. G. Wells' "The Red Room", a big tonal influence and perhaps my favourite ghost story of all time.

The Facts in the Case of Algernon Whisper's Karma

I would not claim that Algernon Whisper is a sane man. I would not even argue the suggestion made in this and other journals that he is criminally insane, for in that regards he has proven himself beyond my ability to defend. I contest only one assertion made by your otherwise reputable periodical: that Algernon is a fool; that his madness is at the expense of his intelligence. Having known the subject since childhood, I write here to state categorically that this is not the case. If anything, Algernon is a genius. He is not the first of his kind to be afflicted by lunacy, nor do I imagine he will be the last. If it is his fate to meet his end by the hangman's noose then so it must be, but let there be no doubt that a great intelligence will be snuffed out in the moment that his life concludes.

I write to address this error for one reason and one only: Algernon Whisper was, and is, my friend.

As I said, I've known Algernon since early childhood, since our schooldays. Even in his youth he was markedly eccentric; but perhaps these things pass unnoticed more easily in a child. For my part, if I observed any signs of strangeness it was only as further evidence to justify my commitment to my friend, for I regarded Algernon with endless approval. He was a source of constant fascination, of ideas both unique and, it seemed to me, impeccably wise. He was also charismatic, witty and remarkable in appearance; he viewed the school's drab uniform with contempt and chose to dress instead, from about the age of seven, in the manner of a man in late middle age. It didn't concern me in the least that I was his only friend, his only sympathiser. Though Algernon's classmates and even his teachers viewed him with evident distrust, I reasoned that this was nothing more than further proof of how detached from the common herd my companion was.

Of course, I could never have imagined then that he would go on to prove me right in so spectacular a fashion.

It was in early adolescence that Algernon came upon the twin infatuations that would lead eventually to his current predicament. I remember both occasions precisely. The first was in his thirteenth year, towards the end of that summer. His father, being wealthy and having a particular fondness for the hunting of big game, would holiday often and for long periods in the most exotic of locales. In this instance, Algernon had just returned from a summer in Africa. He arrived at my home quite unexpectedly and, before I could offer so much as a hello, began to regale me with tales of his latest discovery, with more passion and energy than I'd ever before known him to exhibit.

Whilst his father had been away in search of casualties for his chosen sport, Algernon's curiosity and tedium had led him to begin his own less hostile study of the local wildlife, and he had chanced eventually upon one species that particularly captivated his attentions. These animals were known as meerkats, and were a type of large rodent.

For the rest of the day and late into the evening Algernon narrated to me tales of these creatures' appearance and demeanour, their habitat and particularly of their communal structure. It was this last that really seemed to have inspired him, more than I'd ever known any human society to. He spoke of their democracy of spirit, of true and unfettered egalitarianism, with all the enthusiasm of a revolutionary. I listened, rapt, for it was typical of Algernon that, whatever he spoke of, his enthusiasm was infectious.

I didn't expect this obsession to continue, however.

Algernon constantly found new topics to fascinate him and exhausted each in a matter of days, cramming what to another might require months of study into each brief period. I was surprised when he returned to the subject a week later, and amazed when in a month's time he was still voraciously devouring every text he could find containing the scarcest mention of his cherished meerkats.

As I have said, his fervour never dimmed. I can't begin to guess why this one thing should become such a fascination, favoured over more obvious fields of enquiry, fields in which Algernon's brilliance might have brought limitless benefits to his fellow man. In retrospect, I suppose that it's futile to ask such a question. The greater part of my friend may be rational, but the lesser part is quite mad, and perhaps unintelligible to any other mind.

I noted above that there were two great fixations which, in combination, led to Algernon's current tragedy. The latter occurred three years later almost to the day, and under similar circumstances. Algernon had once again been accompanying his father as he travelled to indulge his bloodthirsty hobby. On this second occasion, as on the first, my friend arrived at my door early in the evening and unanticipated; and again he began to regale me with a new and wondrous discovery. This time he had returned from the mountainous reaches of Tibet, where – left very much to his own devices – he had been making a study of the curious religion of Buddhism, which is commonly practised in that distant land.

Algernon spoke to me then, framed by the doorway and lit by the dying sun at his back, of karma and reincarnation and of many related things. I didn't entirely understand then, nor can I claim to now, for my own intellect has always been trifling in comparison to that of my remarkable friend. The gist, as I saw it, was that each man travels through life accompanied by a spiritual scorecard, on which is tallied every deed he does, whether for good or bad. In his last moments the balance of these is calculated, and this dictates what form he will take when he returns to life – for return he will, not in heaven after the last trumpet as we Christians believe, but as a beast or fowl or insect or perhaps, again, as a man.

As I say, this is only my understanding, and a pale imitation of what Algernon told me that night. I could never hope to capture the intuition or zeal with which he spoke. And once again, I was foolish enough to presume that this was another subject he would rapidly exhaust and abandon. I was wrong, of course. This new study was to become, even more so than the other, the abiding obsession of a lifetime – just as, indirectly, that obsession would help to curtail the life in question.

But I'm ahead of myself, and you might question, reader, how such an innocuous philosophy could lead a man to so heinous a crime. If so, you wonder rightly, for no sane man could have drawn the conclusions that Algernon Whisper did, or have acted so meticulously upon those conclusions.

It was around this time, in fact, that Algernon's incipient madness began to rise to the surface, bubbling up like some underground spring that had long awaited a suitable breach. Still, enchanted as I was by my young companion's genius, I was slow to notice how his logic was becoming steadily less sound. At first things continued between us as they always had. We would meet often, Algernon would lecture, and I would listen keenly, just as I had since early childhood. I was aware of course that he was set increasingly upon a single subject; I might even have acknowledged that day by day it was developing into a monomania. Yet it didn't occur to me that his fascination with the theme of karma and reincarnation differed substantially from the passions he'd indulged in the past.

Even so, I have a definite memory of the point at which his speech first struck me as being especially strange, not merely beyond my own understanding but beyond the common reasoning of mankind. He spoke in hushed tones that night, sat cross-legged on the floor surrounded by books and with his favourite pipe clenched between his teeth, somewhat resembling a portrait of the Buddha which hung on the wall behind him. What he told me was that he had begun to calculate the world's first karmic scale.

"But what on Earth do you mean?" I asked.

"What do I mean? Exactly what I say."

"Algernon," I said, "I'm afraid I don't understand."

He looked back at me with unsettling intensity. "Until now, a man has had no way of telling what end his karma would bring him to. He performs good deeds as well as he can, sometimes he errs, but there's no scheme to it, no deliberateness. He might be reincarnated as a bat or a panda or an ostrich, and it will always be a surprise, the result known only in the moment of reincarnation itself, by which time it's too late to alter or berate his destiny. For thousands of years this fact has gone unchallenged. Well, no more! I have set myself upon the task of creating a qualitative scale of karma and a corresponding rank of reincarnations, so that if a man keeps accurate record and views his actions objectively he may in any moment predict his fate, or alter it if he so wishes."

"But Algernon, is such a thing possible?" I knew in my heart the true answer to my question, and knew equally well what Algernon would reply.

"Is it possible? Of course! Difficult, I grant you, perhaps the vocation of a lifetime, but certainly it's possible. We have, as a beginning, polar extremes: at one end the germ and its kin and at the other, man. The task thenceforward is only of filling in the gaps. There's also the matter of calculating the karmic values of each and every action one might make, but there's already a great bulk of work to assist me in that." He waved vaguely at the books piled haphazardly around the room. "Is it possible? Certainly it is."

I would hope that I didn't look at my friend then as if he were a lunatic, for that would have been unforgivable given the length and depth of our association. I don't doubt, however, that there was something in my expression or tone that gave me away in the conversation that followed. For the more we talked, the colder Algernon became, the more a sense of distance seemed to pry us apart.

By the time I left that evening, my companion would barely bid me goodbye. That moment, as I stepped into the cold evening air, was undoubtedly the end of our close friendship. Thenceforward we would become mere casual companions, and eventually no more than acquaintances. There was nothing abrupt about it, certainly we continued to meet as we always had, and Algernon would enthuse about his grand project in much the same manner he'd always employed, just as I would try to listen with my former enthusiasm. But more and more there were instances when my pretence slipped. He would make the most outrageous statements – "I don't imagine a nun has ever returned to life as an earthworm," or, "What chance, do you think, has the common criminal of being reincarnated as a three-toed sloth?" – and in those moments I was helpless to maintain my attitude of sympathetic enthusiasm, helpless to disguise the thought that I sat in conversation with a madman. On each occasion, I knew that Algernon noticed and I was mortified. I began to avoid him, I think, primarily to escape that feeling of shame, and because I was too much the coward to confront him. If I'd challenged him, had encouraged him to seek help, might he have escaped his current plight? Certainly he might. But I didn't, and it's too late to regret my cowardice now.

Yet it's true as well that our paths diverged, and our friendship became difficult to maintain through no choice of my own. I took a commission in the Great War, and soon after, having escaped that horror courtesy of a minor but disabling wound, I met my wife. Life, in short, led me away from the youth I had shared with Algernon. For his part, he continued his studies, his meagre existence funded by his father's estate.

By the time of our last meeting, we had not seen each other for a year or more. I was astonished when Algernon arrived on my doorstep one chill autumn evening, and all the more amazed to find him so dishevelled and agitated in mood. His state was such that he could hardly greet me; instead he stood with his lips slowly opening and closing and his hands gesticulating abstractly.

"Algernon, what are you doing here? What on Earth's the matter?" I asked – but all the response I received was the whispering of my name in a most pitiful tone. "Come inside," I continued, "Come inside and warm yourself, then tell me what's happened."

I led him into my study, ushered him into the armchair closest the fire and poured generous measures of brandy. Once I felt sure I'd covered every eventuality, I sat opposite him and began again, "What is the matter, Algernon? Tell me, what misfortune has befallen you?"

He sipped at length from his drink, and a little colour returned to his wan cheeks. When eventually he responded, however, his answer remained barely sensible: "No, not misfortune. A mistake, my fault, the fault is all my own."

"Algernon," I said, "You must begin at the beginning. I don't understand you."

He nodded slowly, whilst continuing to sup from his already half-emptied drink. "I have been too good, you see," he said. Then, perhaps realising that this was no more helpful than his previous attempt, he began again. "You know of my project? Of course you do. You've always been kind, though perhaps you haven't always quite believed in me. I can't blame you for that. Perhaps it is the duty of visionaries to be misunderstood by even those who love them most. Well, no matter. You know of my work, but you had no way to know what was in my heart, and I didn't dare tell you for fear you'd think me mad."

I couldn't help flinching at this remark, but Algernon seemed oblivious.

"You're aware too of my fondness for the creatures called meerkats, my respect for their temperament and wise society. Did it occur to you that my other great passion grew from that same source? In Tibet, you see, when I discovered the notions of karma and reincarnation, I saw at once a way in which I might be closer to my beloved meerkats; not merely studying them from afar, through cracked pages and blackened print, but actually dwelling as one of their number. Can you imagine? However pitiful this current life might be, I saw how I might guarantee my happiness in the next. So I began my grand project, my karmic scale, and began at once to follow it myself: to become the rat in my own maze. But oh, I was too hasty. Now I see where my haste and all my wisdom have brought me!"

Parts of this had made sense to me. Parts had illuminated much about my friend that had previously puzzled me. Yet the greater element was nonsense, and so I said again, "I can't understand you, Algernon."

"No... of course you can't," he agreed sadly. "Forgive me my friend, I'm not telling my story plainly enough, and the crucial detail, the crucial mistake, is missing. The key is simply this: I miscalculated. There were flaws in my scale that I have only just discovered and corrected. But far too late... for I have been too good, you see. If I were to die in this instant, I'd be fortunate to return as anything lowlier than a baboon!"

Though I still didn't quite follow, I felt such sympathy for Algernon, who seemed so fragile and defeated, and I was so eager to offer some hope that – fool that I am – I replied without thinking. "But surely then it's just a matter of being less good?"

I realised at once how terrible a thing I'd said. But

before I could correct myself Algernon was on his feet, a curious light illuminating his pale eyes. "Yes, yes. Only I'm very far wrong, and it would take quite a deed to compensate for that..."

He paused then and stared intently at me, as if he could sum me up once and for all with that single glance. Whatever he saw then, it was not what he'd hoped for, for he snatched his coat from the rack, then turned back and said, "We will see each other again soon, no doubt, but for the moment I fear I've imposed enough on your time. I thank you for your hospitality."

He disappeared in the direction of the front door. I was on my feet in an instant and chasing after him into the hall: "Algernon, I didn't mean – Algernon, I hope you aren't thinking..."

"Not at all, my friend," he said, with perfect calm, "and please don't look so worried. You've been kind and understanding and of great help, my oldest ... my only friend."

With those words, he was out the door. I was too baffled and nervous to pursue him further. Perhaps if I had – but no. I might berate myself forever and it would change nothing.

I read in the morning paper about the murder of Tobias Whisper, and my heart sank further with each word, until by the end I was very close to tears. The police had not revealed the name of his killer at that point, and it wasn't until the evening edition that Algernon was implicated. Even then they said only that he had been taken by the constabulary for questioning; his official arrest followed the next day. Details of the affair trickled out at a steady pace after that: how lucid and unrepentant the criminal seemed, how calculated and premeditated the awful crime had been, perhaps the faintest suggestion of irony in some of the lowlier rags at the fact that old Tobias had been assassinated with his own hunting rifle. For the most part, accounts were dreadfully sensational and assumed the most outraged of tones, as is perhaps inevitable for the incomprehensible crime of patricide. Algernon, to my sadness but not to my surprise, received never a word of compassion. In the eyes of press and public alike, he was the most abominable monster. His final words to me seem oddly prescient, for there can be no doubt that but for me he is friendless in this world.

Now that the case of Algernon Whisper is not so fresh and has been replaced in the headlines by new spectacles, I offer this account from the one person who will earnestly mourn his death. It is by no means intended as either explanation or excuse, and I understand that there were other motives to Algernon's crime that perhaps even he himself was not aware of. Tobias Whisper was a cruel and hateful man, who delighted in pain and never to my knowledge showed his son the meanest hint of love. Yet his life was as sacred as any other. Algernon cannot be excused, perhaps he cannot be forgiven, but I hope that in some small way he may be understood.

For my part, I have only one hope for my tale. Let my childhood companion die not as an imbecile but as a great mind lost to the perils of madness, which may take any one of us whether we will it or not.

That is my hope, but my motive is this: Algernon Whisper was, and is, and always shall be, my friend.

~

I'm not proud to admit that I wrote "The Facts in the Case of Algernon Whisper's Karma" on a dare; I'm even less proud to admit that it was a dare I dared myself.

However that's more or less what happened. The core concept – of a man who takes it upon himself to direct the course of his own karmic rebirth, with one very specific goal in mind – came out of a chance remark I made, followed by some bloody-minded part of my brain pointing out that it might conceivably work as a short story, and hey, wasn't that just the perfect reason to give it a go?

With the benefit of experience I would say probably not, no. But as it turned out, it wasn't an altogether terrible idea either. Perhaps the reason was that one concept came together with another, equally odd notion which was then batting around my brain. Or rather, a question: what if Sherlock Holmes was only a genius in John Watson's mind? What if all the crazy was real but the rest of it less so? What if – and I can't be the first Conan Doyle fan to suspect this – it was Watson who was the real brains of the operation, or at least the only one with the requisite number of marbles?

From all of that came a story about friendship and sanity, and the toll that the years can take on both. For something conceived as a joke, it also wound up being quite serious, though of all the stories in the collection this one probably has its tongue wedged most firmly into its cheek.

The Desert Cold

Everyone knows the great desert is hot by day and cold by night. But that heat and cold is something you must experience to understand. The midday sun seems to burn through your eyelids, so that outside the shade you cannot escape; it pricks at your skin like a thousand needles, and sweat offers no relief because you could never sweat enough. It is harsh and cruel, and without water and a good guide you will not live long.

But I had both of those things, and I could weather the days at least. Anticipation, too, had offered some protection. I had arranged my journey hurriedly, I grant you, for I was the victim of circumstance. Yet only a fool goes out upon the sands expecting anything but scalding heat.

The nights, however, were a different matter.

We had been travelling for eight days, my guide and I, and I had carried myself stoically beneath the dreadful sun, which bleaches colour from everything and saps life from the world. I knew well enough to hurry, and not to complain, when my survival depended on our haste.

But when the sun set, when the rocks cooled and cracked and the air became breathable again, then I was afraid. The first night had terrified me; I had been so completely unprepared. There is no cold anywhere on Earth to match the cold of the great desert. It is like death, like the loss of love, a bleakness and a heartbreak. Each following night my fear grew, and by the eighth I could stand no more. I could imagine the chill inside my bones, I could conceive of no strength that would resist it. That fear must have shown – in my step, my posture, my face.

I think I would have died then if he'd let me. His name was Harad, and his skin was tanned almost black from countless treks across the sand. He had said so very little throughout our journey that I was startled when he spoke.

"It is not weakness," he said, "but a lack of perspective."

I didn't understand, of course, and I stared at him foolishly.

"You are afraid of the night's cold?"

There was no good in denying it. "Yes," I admitted, "I am very afraid."

He stopped abruptly and stared into my eyes. His face was expressionless, except for his gaze, which was as hypnotic as a hawk's. "Your thinking is wrong. It will kill you."

"How so?"

"The cold is nothing. It is the absence of the day's heat, no more. If you lose something that will soon return, you have lost nothing at all. Do you understand?"

I nodded hesitantly.

Now, a week later, a stranger amidst the comforts of a strange town, and with the great desert only a memory, I ask myself the same question: did I understand? Do I understand now? I know that I fear the desert and that I could not cross it again. Yet it is an undeniable truth that I am still alive to write this.

But despite the blaze in the hearth, I remember that cold still; I can sense it among the dunes, like a beast that waits for me. And the spirit I left there will seek its vengeance as well, should I ever try to return. He was old and patient, and his shade will be the same. If it cannot take me in life then it will find me in the grave.

Still, I have gained perhaps a little understanding of my own. Harad was more astute than I, for he had survived a hundred treks through that barren place protected by his truth. But I am here, alive and safe before my fire, while he lies dead beneath the sands that he made his home.

He was protected from the cold, it is true, but not from a knife between the shoulder blades. He will not return home to guide my enemies, and no other knew my course.

I grieve for my family, on whom vengeance will surely have been exacted in my absence. I grieve for my first crime, which has left me an exile, fleeing the punishment of death and left to live with a fate that is barely kinder. But more, in this instant of writing, I grieve for Harad, who was a good companion, a good guide, a wise and fearless man.

If one were to follow his own logic then perhaps there is nothing so terrible in death. For death is no more than the absence of life; and life, it may be, is something we shall return to, just as the sun rises by dawn and sheds new warmth on the earth.

I wish that this might be true; but I am no philosopher, only a petty criminal of some little notoriety and wealth. Whatever my hopes or fears, they are neither knowledge nor truth, and I can say with certainty only this of Harad:

For all his wisdom, for all his fearlessness, his bones still lie frozen now in the cold of the desert night.

~

"The Desert Cold" was my first ever professional sale, almost seven years ago now, and to the then fairly new webzine Flash Fiction Online *– still going strong to this day, incidentally.*

I was still finding my way back then, more than a little blindly, and this slender tale came together by a long and awkward route: it began as a vignette, more of a scene-setting exercise than a story, which would become the core of the first two thirds of the finished piece. I came back to it much later, in a completely different – and much darker! – frame of mind, and what had been an atmospheric episode turned into an ugly study of how quickly human beings can abandon their best intentions when their own skins are on the line.

The War of the Rats

22nd June 1916
My Dearest Emily,

Oh, with what a range of emotions I read your last! Joy to begin with, of course, for as often as I say it, still, you can hardly believe what a pleasure it is to hear from you. But imagine, won't you, when one's days are taken up with drudgery, with the endless roar of the shelling, and all in all this dreadful back-and-forth business of men trying to kill each other, what it is to receive word from a fond wife!

Happiness, then, but quickly followed by the most frightful guilt, to realise I'd worried you so badly, and then an overwhelming tenderness as I came to the part where you said... Well, I'm sure you remember, and suffice to say that I've never felt so cared for as I did to read that last paragraph of yours. Truly, it was almost worth taking a wound and putting such a fright into you to read such lovely sentiments.

Still, my darling, however nice it is to hear and however it might buoy me for a while, you mustn't worry. I'm safe enough now, and soon I'll be back on the line, where I'll be a hundred times more careful for this little caution of a wound. Then I'll see out the rest of this sorry war, which will be done by autumn if it lasts that long, and after that I'll be back with you. I'll return to writing my plays, which I confess I miss almost as much as I do your pretty face, and we shall have our long put-off honeymoon. A Christmas honeymoon, how's that? We'll pick up our life just where we left off, and never speak of Germany or war or any painful thing again. Do you believe me? Well you must!

Now that that's said, I suppose I must tell you the details; that is, the facts of it, unlike that panicked, self-pitying note I sent you last. Well, it was Forsythe and I, and we'd gone over into No-Man's-Land to pull out a lad, one of our snipers, whose spotter was shouting that the boy had taken a nasty hit. We were dashing as well as we could through the dark and rain, with the filthy ground sucking at our feet, when all of a sudden I heard a whistle and felt something prick my leg – just a sharp sting, like an insect bite.

I was ready to carry on, but I found suddenly that I couldn't stand. So I toppled over, splashing in the mud. All I could think was what I must have looked like to Forsythe. I tried to tell him I was all right, but then I looked down at my leg, and despite that thick darkness I could see the blood. Still, even then I couldn't take it altogether seriously. "Will you look at that?" I said.

It seemed quite a pickle at first, for our sniper was hit as badly as or worse than I was; it was no good to have Forsythe hauling me back. He made a few noises in that direction and I told him, no, I can still crawl, can't I? I meant it, too, for we weren't so far from our own front. Forsythe tried to argue, but I'd have none of it, and in the end he wished me luck and set off again, leaving behind the stretcher we'd hauled all that way.

As I watched Forsythe creep off, as he was absorbed into the darkness, I realised finally what I'd set myself up for. My leg was starting to hurt by then; just an ache, but with a pinch to it that warned me how much worse it was going to get. Already I felt muddled. I imagined crawling on my face through the mud, dragging one useless leg, until I tumbled into the enemy's trenches, or else strung myself up on their wire.

I gave it a few minutes. Just as I'd thought, the pain began to worsen. After a while, it occurred to me that I was probably in shock, and that if I left it much longer I might not be able to move at all. I did my best to focus, to remember which way we'd come from, taking the angle of our discarded stretcher as a clue.

Getting started was the hardest part. Almost as soon as I'd set off I thought I could make out our lines, a stripe across the near horizon. Our wire, which has been so often torn and restrung and jumbled with debris, looked like something that had grown of its own accord – a strange thought when I knew nothing could thrive in that long-poisoned earth. I tried to keep it in view as I crawled, pressed flat on my belly. The mud here smells something awful, like a swamp and a charnel house at once. It's no wonder, for the land has become both of those things and worse. But I could hardly bear the stink in my nostrils and very much wanted to try to stand, damn my hurt leg and the risk of another bullet. Still worse was the thought of what I might be creeping over, what I might reach out and touch. The risk of getting caught on the wire seemed the least of it. So many men had died out there, so many had been left to the worms and the rats. There in the darkness, alone, I was horribly afraid of crawling into one of them.

So it was that, having made my way back through our defences and knowing I must be somewhere close to our front trench, I screamed for all I was worth when I felt fingers brush my outstretched wrist. I think I must have been a little unhinged by then.

Immediately a brisk voice called out, "Be quiet!" Then the fingers closed around my wrist, pulled me forward, and someone I couldn't see said, redundantly, "Get him down here!" For by then I was half over and, before I could help it, tumbling hard onto the fire step. There was much grunting and groaning, not all on my part, before the man who'd hauled me managed to extricate himself.

"Barrister?" he said. "Is that you?"

This time, I identified the voice. It was Winters, our sergeant; a gruff old sod, but I was glad to recognise him just then. "It is, it's Barrister," I mumbled. "Took one in the leg, but it's all right now."

"All right, is it?" he said. "I bet they heard you caterwauling all the way to Berlin."

It seems funny now. I suppose, in a grim sort of way, it was then. At any rate, I felt relieved. And Winters was a sport, for all his hard words... seeing I couldn't walk, he had another stretcher brought up and ordered a couple of lads to take me back to the Dressing Station.

After they'd made a go of bandaging my wound I spent the rest of the night there, sunk in a fitful sleep. The next morning, about sunrise, two more men came to carry me on to the rest area. I didn't know it then, but there'd been some fighting further up the line, and the hospital was jam-packed. I was left in a tent with a great many other fellows, most of them worse off than I was, and so I passed the rest of that day. It was then that I sent you my last letter, when I was still, I think, delirious. Looking back, I can't imagine how I even managed to put pen to paper, or to persuade one of the orderlies to carry it to the post for me... and I can only think, with horror, of how you must have felt to read it.

Now it's a couple of days later, and although they haven't found time to do any proper work on my leg – a scratch compared with some of the horrors they're dealing with – they've cleaned me up and made me comfortable, which is all I could sensibly ask. I haven't heard what came of Forsythe and our sniper; it's hard to get word here. I hope they made it back.

Looking over what I've written, I see I've used up an inordinate amount of the paper you sent me, and gone into more detail than I'd meant to. I reassure myself with the knowledge that you are a sensible and modern woman who won't cringe at talk of wounds and such – and that you'll trust me when I say, once more, that all will be right in the end.

Until then, with love,
Your Fred

23rd June 1916
My Dearest Emily,

Funny to be writing again when I know you won't have had my last yet. Oh well! The truth is, I had an awful fright last night, and since it would seem silly to anyone here and I can't resist the need to tell someone, I'm telling it to you. For that I can only apologise, and hope once more that you won't get yourself down with worry, when I assure you that – with daylight to dispel my night terrors – I am my usual, cheerful self once more.

Let me start by saying that the hospital – which the army calls a Casualty Clearing Station, but what a mouthful that is! – is actually an old French school house. The building has taken its share of shelling, as everywhere has, and there are holes in the roof and walls; but they've made a good effort of tidying the place, and all told it's a damn sight better than even the nicest of dugouts. They've moved me inside now and given me a bed, which is actually a mattress and blankets, for the few real beds are reserved for the severe cases. Still, it's pleasant to have upright walls around me, softness beneath my back, and an air of normality that one can scarcely imagine when one lives like an animal in the ground. When the guns are quiet I can almost imagine myself in our bedroom, resting before breakfast on a Sunday morning.

Nevertheless, there are limits to what they can do, with so many wounded always coming in and so many sick. They are panicked and weary, these medical men, though in a different way from those of us at the Front: they look constantly harassed. There are simply not enough of them to go around, and they know it as well as we do. One must make allowances, and I've tried to these past days, though my leg has given me a deal of pain.

All in all, then, I was thankful yesterday evening when a nurse came to tell me they'd be working on my wound that night. "Better late than never," she told me, with forced cheer.

My good leg is taking the weight of my bad one, so she had an orderly lend me a shoulder and hoist me where I needed to go, which was up a flight of stairs and into a little room just down from the main ward. The smaller room had been made out in a fair semblance of an operating theatre; I swear I've seen worse back home. There was another man there, fiddling with some equipment, and a surgeon whom I saluted, assuming him to be an officer.

"No need for all that," he said. "Just lie down and make yourself comfortable."

I did as I was told, as best I could.

"I'm going to have to dig around a little," the surgeon told me, and his tone was so upright and unquestionable that I hardly thought to worry at what he was saying. "It's all right, though," he went on. "This chap," – and he motioned to the other man – "is going to give you something for the pain."

The other man came over, hauling his equipment with him. It consisted of a metal tank, that clanked as he moved, and great lengths of hosing, with a mask at the end of the hose that he held before him. "We're out of novocaine," he said. "So I'm going to put you under. More than that little nick warrants, you understand, but at least you can have a decent nap."

I can't say why, but that was the first moment I felt any apprehension, seeing that mask lower towards my face and catching the musty odour of rubber mingled with the petrol stink of ether. Perhaps it reminded me too strongly of that other gas, which has grown all too familiar along the trenches. At any rate, I tried to turn my head. He knew his business, though, for I'd hardly thought it before he had the mask on me. I heard a thin hiss and tried to protest, when all of a sudden I discovered it was impossible to put my thoughts into words.

Then darkness swarmed down over me, as though some gloomy mass had seeped out of the ceiling. I could still make out both the surgeon and the anaesthesiologist, but they were alarming figures, gaunt and crooked. Though I could hear them speaking, their words were reduced to a dull bass tremble, conversation echoing from a distant room. I wanted badly to complain, to explain that something had gone wrong.

Someone fumbled at the temporary bandages around my leg. The sensation was distant, like a memory of old pain; yet somehow that made it worse. I was too drugged to resist, not so drugged that I couldn't feel what was going on – nor understand what it meant. I knew what was about to happen.

Knowing didn't prepare me. Not for the coldness of metal probing the ripped meat of my calf. Not as I felt the blade slice inside me, rasping upon bone. I was still detached, experiencing it as though it were being described to me in the minutest detail. The pain, in itself, wasn't so bad. What troubled me was my helplessness. If I could only make my lips move, my throat work, and croak out one word then it might all be over. But I couldn't. I could only lie there and endure.

Eventually the scalpel-work was done. Then came the needle and thread. That was better in a way, for it signalled an approaching end, but worse in that my numbness was beginning to wear off. Now I could move my fingers, my lips, just barely. And, without my control, my leg had begun to twitch every time the needle went in – until eventually the surgeon noticed.

"Hello, what's this?" he asked, addressing the anaesthesiologist I presumed.

There came a muffled answer.

"Well, keep him still," the surgeon said, his voice oddly slow and drawling. "If he's thrashing around he'll tear these stitches."

Fingers clamped around my leg and the stitching began again. At least the surgeon worked quickly; though the ordeal seemed to last an age, it couldn't have been more than a minute or two. I knew, somehow, which stitch was the last, and wanted to sigh with relief – but I couldn't even make my numbed mouth do that much.

"Make sure he's kept still," the surgeon said again, "I won't have him messing up all my work."

I felt myself being moved then, carried, and I caught vague impressions of space, made cloudy by the anaesthetic: what might have been a door frame, the angle of a ceiling – though improbably abrupt – and then an impossible expanse of room around me, as though the walls had receded to an unreachable horizon. Then I was on a bed, and I thought my whole body would melt with the comfort of it.

Even when the shadowy figures who had deposited me began to tuck me firmly in place with blankets I considered myself fortunate. I was at rest; I was warm, and the pain had receded to a hesitant throb. Let them immobilise me if it pleased them. With the drug still in my system, I had neither desire nor agency to move anyway. Very soon I was drifting into a woolly sleep that even the nag of pain and the unpleasantness of my experience under the knife couldn't resist.

I woke with a start. Despite the blankets tight around me, I was cold. My head hurt, and felt stuffed with cotton. My mouth was achingly dry. I thought about crying out for a drink of water, but it was pitch dark, and in any case I found it was still difficult to work my jaw. However much time had passed, I was still suffering from the effect of the anaesthetic.

As more of consciousness ebbed into my tired, drugged brain, I became sure something had woken me. But at first I couldn't identify what. I racked my memory, trying to separate out the detritus of half-recollected nightmares, fractured episodes that seemed to consist of little more than motion and shadow.

Then I heard it, and knew without doubt what had dragged me from the depths: a squeaking, shrill and curious-sounding. I wondered that everyone hadn't woken, it seemed so loud. Immediately, my skin began to prickle. My blood was like ice.

You know better than anyone, Emily, how afraid I am of rats. Ever since that thing when I was a boy, the time I got locked in the cellar, the very thought of them has filled me with dread. Yet here in France, where the ground has been broken and churned, where there's so much for them to feed upon, they are everywhere; they live like kings. Even in the hospital, though the staff do their best, the vermin can't be kept out.

There was nothing for a while, no sound except the distant shelling. I wondered if I might have imagined it. Then, straining my ears, I caught a new sound. It was the rustle of heavy fabric, coming from the foot of my bed – and even as I heard it, I felt the tremble of motion, the swish of coarse fur against my foot.

I wanted to scream. Oh, how badly I wanted to. I could make no sound. I could twitch my calf a little, but that did nothing to dislodge the thing creeping beside it. I felt the brush of little feet, of whiskers, against my bare skin. Though there surely should have been men snoring, sobbing in their sleep, though I should been able to hear the distant guns, the night was so quiet that I could make out the snuffle of its breath.

A rat. A rat! The word chimed in my mind. It was all the sense I could make of the situation. *There is a rat*, my hysterical thoughts protested uselessly, *crawling up my leg.* Yet behind that immediate, enormous fear – so huge that it seemed to eclipse even the possibility of sensible thought – there lay another, deeper terror. I just couldn't, wouldn't admit it to myself.

The motion stopped. The whiskers gave a slow,

exploratory twitch. I knew what it had found; what it had been seeking all along. Oh god ... I'd have given anything for the strength to just kick my leg. Here was that profoundest fear, which I'd been unable even to acknowledge until then. For he was at my bandage. Sniffing. Nuzzling.

I've seen the way they get at dead men, Emily. A wound to them is nothing but an entrance to somewhere warm and safe, or else a place to eat. That was the terror I could hardly let myself think of. Whenever I'd seen rats scurrying about the dead I'd gone profoundly cold, averted my eyes and clammed up for a while, sinking into a sort of stupor. I'd always counted myself lucky that my reaction had gone unnoticed.

Now there was no hiding. No stupor would protect me. I heard his teeth before I felt anything, a tender chatter interspersed with pauses that seemed almost thoughtful. As he continued to work, however, I could feel the pressure of his head, as when a dog pushes for attention. He toiled with steady determination. He knew what he was looking for, and knew that with patience he'd have it.

Soon I could feel my bandage coming loose. He had prised up a corner to pick at the folds below. Somewhere underneath my fear I couldn't help a sense of awful fascination; there was something interesting in his steady efforts. Experienced as sensation alone, it wasn't unlike the surgeon's labours, and in my confused thoughts the two began to run together. But while the surgeon had picked at my flesh to heal me, I knew my intimate companion wished me no good at all.

Finally he'd managed to get his snout under a flap of bandage. He paused, to inspect his work maybe, or to take the measure of his success – though it seemed to me a deliberate protraction of my torment. Even without the anaesthetic's effects, I was rigid, almost senseless with fear.

He gave a soft little squeak. His whiskers brushed raw flesh. Then he moved in once more.

Sharp rodent teeth picked at a stitch, sending a shudder of pain all through me – and with that, it was as though a spell had broken. Suddenly I could move, as if my utter terror had boiled away the last dregs of the anaesthetic. The moment I knew I could use my lungs I put them straight to work, making the most horrendous racket you've ever heard. Finding my legs once more mobile I flung them about, trying to tear myself from the clinging blankets, or to tip myself to the floor if that was what it took.

It wasn't long before a light came on and an orderly rushed in. He caught hold of my shoulders and pinned me down. I'd almost worn myself out by then, and hadn't any strength left to try and throw him off. In any case, with the light on and other patients roused from their own suffering, my panic was giving way to a cold sense of shame. I gave up altogether when he told me roughly, "Calm down, man, it's only a bad dream."

Now, in the daylight, I wonder if he was right. I'd thrashed so much that I'd made my wound bleed, and they changed my bandages before I could check for bite marks. I saw no scraps of fur or droppings amongst my blankets. Could I have imagined it all? I've known men to see the strangest things, to rant at nightmares with their eyes open and in broad daylight. This war has a knack for breaking men down, for plucking out their darkest fears for all to see.

Well, nightmare or no, I am sane enough to not mix up night terrors with reality. And I shall stay that way... for I've the thought of you to keep me intact, my love, and to remind me of what it is I'm fighting for.

Reading back over what I've written, I realise how grotesque it sounds! Well, it *was* grotesque, and I'm not ashamed to tell you how sorely frightened I was... more than I'd been since I arrived in France, more than I've ever been in battle. But it's over and done with, and what's more, I'll have peace and quiet for a week or two now, while I get myself better. So you see, it would be silly of you to worry about me, and you should concentrate instead on looking forward to the day when we see each other again,

With love,
Your Fred

25th June 1916
Dearest Emily,

I've just read your letter, and now am feeling the need to write back straight away, lest I forget some of what I want to tell you.

Sad to say, my news is a disappointment; not dreadful, you understand, and no one's to blame, but nor is it the reassurance I might have hoped to give you.

I was called in today to see the captain who'd worked on my leg. He has made an office in one of the school rooms, which must have been a little library or something similar, for the wall behind his battered desk was shelved and the shelf still full of books. Some of them were in French, and left over from its past life, I presumed, but others were in English, medical texts by the look.

It was the most incongruous thing you can imagine. Many a time I've been struck by some relic of the old world, left intact by the guns and the upheaval... a little flower garden in a demolished village we passed through, a group of children playing in another village that had all but been evacuated, a cat lounging upon the bonnet of a broken-down truck not a mile from the Front... but nothing quite struck me as sharply as that bookcase did. It was as though the Captain had, through sheer force of will, kept intact a part of his life in England, preserving it like a fly in amber.

As I was staring, however, I caught another surprise. For I was sure I saw something move; two, three, four books trembled and returned to their places, as if motion behind them had jarred them for a moment out of place. I wanted to look more carefully, for it was hard to make out; but I realised then that the Captain was observing me. Remembering his earlier advisement that I not stand to attention, I asked instead, "It's not a Blighty, then?" I tried to sound cheerful, but I couldn't help thinking of you as I said it.

"Hardly," he said, not looking up from his reading. "No, if you take care of that leg then you'll be back to normal within a month. I'll write you a letter telling them to keep you off active duty. Still, I'd have liked to keep you longer."

I tried to give him my full attention, and not to look at the bookcase. It was difficult, for again the books were moving: a whole section now, where a dozen volumes in brown leather sat together. Carefully, trying to keep the quaver out of my voice, I said, "Not much space, eh?"

"No," he said, "quite." Then he returned his gaze conspicuously to the papers on his desk. I wondered if he meant for me to leave. I was ready to, except that I couldn't keep my eyes from gravitating back to the bookcase. Now, where the books had been moving, I thought I could make out a shape in the shadows. As I watched, it moved, with a horrible little jerking motion.

"We just can't keep a bed for every man," the Captain said, oblivious to what was going on behind his head. "They tell me it's to get worse... far worse."

He sounded dejected; strained, in fact, to the very point of breaking. But for the incident which had given me such a fright, I'd been enjoying my time in the hospital, and I decided I should say something cheerful to reassure him.

Yet just as I was about to speak, the words caught in my throat – so thoroughly that I thought I'd have to vomit if I'd ever utter another syllable. For the thing in the bookcase, the black thing twitching in the shadows, had turned its gaze my way. A pair of pinprick eyes fixed upon me: red eyes, beady and bright, staring with a mix of hate and impudence.

The captain picked that moment to look up – and there was concern in his voice as he said, "Are you all right, man?"

I wanted to tell him what was occurring behind his shoulder, but what could I possibly say? *'Sir, you should know there's a rat in your bookcase.'* "Of course, sir," I mumbled, instead.

I looked back at the bookcase. There was nothing to see now; nothing moving, no despising red eyes. The books sat still and in their places, as though they'd never been disturbed.

I threw the captain a salute – for as much as he might not care for such things, he was a damn sight more of an officer than some I've met – and then I took my leave, as quickly as I could with a crutch and a gammy leg. For strange as it is to tell, Emily, I knew it was the same rat, the one that had preyed upon me in the night. And I knew it had been looking at me – at me specifically.

You must think me very silly, and perhaps I am. Fear works upon you over here in a way I could never have imagined at home. It's so hard to resist when one has every reason to be afraid. Yet there are worse things than the vermin: shells and the laugh of the machine guns, sniper's bullets and gas, and none of those have worked upon my nerves as the events of the last twenty-four hours have.

Tonight will be my last day in the hospital. Tomorrow I head back to the trenches. Perhaps that will shake me out of this funk I find myself in; perhaps real and undeniable dangers will keep me from regurgitating childhood terrors and fussing over nightmares. In the meantime, write often, please, as often as you can bear ... for there are so few true comforts out here, you know, and not one to match your letters,

With love,
Your Fred

28th June 1916
Dearest Emily,

So I'm back... Back with my company, at any rate, for they'd been pulled from the fire trench in the days since my accident and are now held in reserve. I suppose that's why I was moved here at all; not even the army would send a man incapable of standing to fight or hold the line. I'm probably as safe here as I would be back in the hospital, for the only real risks are shelling and sickness, and I was as vulnerable to those there as I am here.

Sad to say, no one seems glad to see me. Oh, my mates made a show of it, but they soon gave in to glumness. We'd been told before I took my hit that it would be rest rather than another spell in reserve, and yet here we are, and the rumour going round is that there's worse on the way: a push coming, today or tomorrow, before the end of the week at any rate. The prospect hangs over us like a pall. Everyone knows it's going to be something big, and me more than most, for the fact that I'm here when I'm no good for fighting means they must be expecting our back lines to fill at a damned fast rate.

I showed Winters the letter the Captain gave me, thinking all the while that he might countermand it or refer it up to our CO; for though he's not a bad man, he is without doubt a hard one, and I knew he wouldn't like having a soldier lollygagging. However, all he did was give it the quickest of once-overs and say, "So that's it, is it, Barrister? Well, keep your head down. Don't get in the way of fighting men."

That little reprimand stung, I confess. I feel useless. There are not many jobs even in a support trench that one can do while hobbling on crutches. I'm keeping to a dugout mostly, and no one is very concerned with my absence. Shall I describe it? Think of a small space, walls hacked from the raw dirt, roof reinforced with sheet metal – though a direct hit would certainly return the whole place to the earth. As a living space, it's devoid of even the meanest luxury, barely fit for the habitation of men, and except for evenings I have it mostly to myself, for the rest are out on duty. Out here it's the company that keeps you going more than anything, and I've had precious little of that.

No, I tell a lie: I'm never quite alone, however I might wish to be. For there's no escaping the rats. They make their homes here as though we had dug our holes and passages entirely for their benefit; as though we'd only entered into this war to lay the groundwork for their empire. There are rat villages in the walls, rat towns... I believe there must be whole rat nations. If I didn't despise them so, I suppose I'd have to admire their industry.

Until this last week, I'd found that their ever-presence had inured me somewhat against my phobia. When I first arrived they bothered me terribly, as so much of this new life did, and then my disgust turned by degrees into something like forbearance. However bothersome a thing is, it is hard to be really unnerved when one sees it everywhere and all the time.

Yet after my recent experience I find that familiarity does little to blunt my fear. Even now, as I write, they are running about the floor, quite oblivious to my being here. If someone else comes in they'll scamper, but so long as it's just me they act as if this space belongs to them alone. Every so often one will even clamber over me, and I flap to drive it off – for however much I despise them, I find myself too soft-hearted to do them real harm.

At any rate, my hand-waving doesn't bother them. They flop in the air and land on their feet and carry on about their business. They care nothing for men, do you see? Perhaps they have the foresight to know that soon we will be most of us dead; perhaps while we're moving around and cursing at and molesting them in whatever ways we can, they overlook our efforts as a temporary inconvenience. Out here, they are greater than we – in numbers, in strength, in attitude. I suspect sometimes they have a wider perspective that we lack.

So I watch them, telling myself it's a sort of study, an amusement to pass the invalid hours ... but really I think I'm growing a little obsessed. This letter, most likely, proves as much. How sorry I am to waste words on such nonsense, words which surely could be better spent. How I wish I had something good to tell you, some glimmer of hopeful news. But there is none. There's only dull pain, the thunder of the shelling and the rats.

With love,
Your Fred

1st July 1916
Dear Emily,

Yet again I've given you no time to reply. I haven't had one back from you, in fact, since I left the hospital. Perhaps the post has yet to catch up with me. I hope it's that and not that I've upset you. I know how you can be quiet when I've worried you too much; how you'd go for days sometimes hardly saying a word as you picked over some doubt. Oh Emily, if I've set you fretting and put you off writing then I can only be sorry and crave your understanding. I need you, my love. Even if it's only your words, made cold by ink and paper, I need you with me now.

Still, if the worst has happened and all my dismal talk has made you too sick of me to write, then I find that I can't blame you. Yet nor can I bring myself to stop. I confess that these letters are more for my benefit than your happiness, for I'm sure they offer little enough of that. But Emily, I have no one here to confide in, and this wound has made me lonely – lonely and yet unable to ever be alone. It's a limited sort of friendship that one finds here, where nothing better is allowed, yet I miss it badly. And in the meantime I am cursed with a surplus of dumb animal company, crawling, creeping company that shows me no regard at all.

Has it only been two days since I wrote? Time passes slowly. Our patch of trench is dizzy with a sense of preparation, and still there's nothing concrete: the fighting goes on further up the line, we hear wild reports and the tattoo of the big guns, as though the very sky were a drum-skin being beaten, and the coughing of far-off machine guns in every quiet gap... all of this has been constant, and they say we might be moved up at any hour, yet there's not one definite word.

The other men are skittish and quarrelsome, when I see them at all. Apart from me and the others wounded, no one has seen much rest these last two months. I think they resent me and my little scratch, though no one says as much. Who could blame them? For my part, I worry what will become of me when we're caught in the push, as is surely only a matter of time, and then feel mean and small for thinking of myself. It is one thing to face danger, to confront it with one's eyes open; it's another, and worse I think, to sit in its shade for weeks and months on end.

But while little happens in the world of men, the hours are frantic indeed in that other kingdom busying itself beside our own. I fear I'm becoming something of an expert: perhaps when I return home I shall put aside my play-writing to become an authority of rodent behaviour; or maybe I shall merely forgo the petty theatre of human lives in favour of new and yet smaller subjects. For rats, too, have their dramas, their friendships, their tribulations and their discords.

That last most of all. Perhaps they have been learning from their landlords. For as I've watched I've come to appreciate that there's a conflict raging, of which my miserable dugout is perhaps only one battlefield.

It was yesterday when I observed a first, important detail: there is a hierarchy amongst the rats. For a while their behaviour seemed chaotic, a competition in which each fended for himself. Yet after a time my eyes kept picking out one beast in particular, whose fur is a peculiar brown that might almost be called red. He's distinctive-looking, at any rate, and whenever he's out the others are careful. They give him space, which they never do for each other, and I've even seen them give up scraps of food. He reminds me of some ancient warlord, a Genghis Khan of vermin.

But he is not alone. Late this afternoon I was introduced to his opposing number. It was a raid, as bold an endeavour as I've seen: there must have been fifty of them, and all in a cluster they burst under the gas blanket, chattering and gnashing their teeth. At their front was a great black creature, fully an inch longer than any of the rest. He had a scar over half his head, where the fur had not grown back, which gave him rather a piratical air. All in all, he was a different sort of leader than his red counterpart, a general not afraid to get his paws dirty.

For all that, his raid was over almost before it started... A mere skirmish, with a few cuts and scrapes on either side but few real casualties. They made very much noise about it, but I concluded that the black rat was merely testing his neighbour's defences, ready for a greater push later. After it was done, silence reigned for a while; silence, at least, in the rat world, for of course there are no pauses in the sounds of human war. The wounded retreated to wherever it is they go, the burrows that must exist somewhere within the walls of our own subterranean warrens. The dead were left where they fell.

Emily... Write soon, will you? If I should find a way to send this, if it should wend its way across the Channel and if you should ever receive it, write as soon as you can. I need your calm words. I'm scared of the way my mind wanders.

Please, write to me soon.

Love,
Fred

2nd July 1916
Dear Emily,

Why haven't I heard from you? I suppose there's no post being delivered anywhere on the line, with everything in such an uproar, but nevertheless, I'm afraid. Have I really put you off? Have I made you hate me, or brought you to such a fright that you won't put pen to paper? I can't believe it, for you've always been so strong – much stronger than I. Perhaps if you were here you could even bear it, where I start to think I cannot.

Everyone is gone now and I'm alone. It happened during the night. The nearest guns had been raging for twenty-four hours; they are never quiet, not for long, but this time they wouldn't pause, and our earth walls shivered with the sound – as if the entire world has become a a noise and nothing else. It was beyond all endurance, and we cowered through the dark hours like children in a storm.

There were a dozen of us in here, a space barely suited to four. Two of them, men I know by name but little else, were sitting on my bunk, so that I had to pull my leg up, which hurt like all damnation. They smoked and drank foul-tasting tea and cursed at each other for no reason, when they weren't drummed into silence by the remonstrance of the guns. I've never in my life been so glad of human companionship.

Now they are gone. The rest of the company are to make their way up to the front, to reinforce the men already there, and sometime around dawn they'll go over into No-Man's-Land. Meanwhile, I have my own orders. I am to wait until evening and then, if my company aren't returned, make my own way back to the support trenches.

Winters told me candidly that I'd have a struggle on my hands if it comes to that, for they're expecting a steady stream of wounded, and new men coming up all the while. "Don't make a nuisance of yourself," he said. "There'll be plenty worse off than you." He was outwardly himself, gruff and hard-worded, but there was a look in his eyes as he talked that I'd never thought to see there. He didn't believe he was coming back. He's a strong man through and through, but there's no strength that can endure here. This war is a furnace that burns weak and strong alike, which melts courage like tallow. I don't think I'll see Winters again. I don't know if I'll see any of them.

I can hear the fighting. It doesn't sound so very far away. I can't tell who's winning or losing... if those words mean anything any more. What would it mean to win this war? Should we march into Berlin? Arrest the Kaiser? For us here, the only victory would be an end – an immediate, bloodless end. But the noises I hear are of violence, of spitting bullets, of explosions that can vaporise flesh – of the machine of war threshing men like corn.

Meanwhile, in my dugout, another war has been raging. I was right: the black rat's intrusion yesterday was no more than a probing of his enemy's defences. Today they came in earnest. How can I describe this? It was as if the walls and floors had come alive. First a roar like a great ocean swell, the patter and splash of thousands of feet, and a terrible noise made out of endless tiny shrieks. And then they came, a living wave, dark bodies churning over each other, too many to count. They flowed through the entrance, across the floor – and were met by enemies beyond number in an opposing flood, from the walls and from every dark recess.

My heart rose into my mouth.

I'd never seen such violence. The savagery of men seemed as nothing compared with the ferocity of nature. I had heard Tennyson's 'red in tooth and claw', but I'd never understood until then. What need had beasts of guns and bombs and shells? I watched creatures no bigger than my foot tear each other apart, literally into pieces, in mobs and in single combat. Blood flowed like water, spattered like rain. The dead piled in mounds and were trampled underfoot. The wounded were picked out and destroyed.

And throughout, the two generals clung to the sidelines: the black rat and the red. They scampered and shrieked; sometimes they even fought themselves, but never against any animal bigger than they, and often just to pick off an injured straggler. I wondered how they could make any sense of the struggle, how they told one side from the other. Perhaps they didn't, and the rules of vermin war were fundamentally, incomprehensibly different from our own.

Or perhaps, I thought, it wasn't so different after all. If I could see the war of men raging outside from such a vantage point, would there be any distinction between English and German? They fought and died the same. They would all of them rather be somewhere else, rather be safe with their loved ones. No one would choose to be torn to shreds by bullets or to drown in thigh-deep mud. No one who had known it would ever choose this war if it wasn't chosen for them.

I don't know how long the battle of the rats raged on for, but it ended as suddenly as it had begun. The survivors departed the ways they'd come, some via the gas blanket, others retreating into the hidden spaces in the walls. No ground, so far as I could judge, had been won, no battle lines amended. But there were very many dead.

I sat there in bed, back rigid, cold sweat beading my brow. My fear had transformed into something else, a numbness that reached to my bones. Slowly I realised that the sounds of human battle had diminished too, faded to something like their usual clamour. It did nothing to make me feel better. I stared at the newly-carpeted dirt floor, tried to make sense of its ragged patches of brown and black and crimson. I stared, I don't know for how long. It was as though fear had insulated me from the wider world, locked me inside this vignette of violence and death.

Then, as if from nowhere, I heard footsteps on the duckboards outside, and a moment later a head appeared through the gas blanket. I gained an impression of hair greying at the wings, of pocked and sallow skin; a face I dimly recognised. Seeing me there in my bunk, he asked, "What's this?"

That brought me round. I found my shivering had stopped without my noticing. Even my hands were perfectly still. I pulled the blankets back to show him the bandages around my leg. It seemed a weak enough answer, but he accepted it.

He came inside then, and I saw he was a sergeant. He didn't appear to notice the torn and blood-slicked bodies scattered about, though they fairly paved the ground; from the waxen cast of his face and the distant look in his eyes, I guessed he'd seen too much death that day to bother himself with a little more.

Thinking I should say something, I asked, "How has it gone?"

"A bloody massacre," he said, sounding both distracted and matter-of-fact. "Half of us are dead, or stuck out there. No way to get anyone back in until night falls."

I asked if he knew a Sergeant Winters, and whether he'd made it.

"Winters?" he said. "I think I saw him near the start, at the front of a little crowd. They were going for one of the machine guns; it ripped them up like paper. If that's your man I wouldn't expect to hear from him again."

Written down, his words sound callous, but there was no cruelty in the way he said it, just a terrible weariness.

"If anyone else comes this way," he went on, "send them down the line. We're trying to get everyone together and make some sense of it." He sounded as if he didn't have much faith in either prospect. He ducked out, and I heard his sloshing steps fade up the trench.

I thought of Winters, and realised I could find no emotion in myself either. Probably he was dead. Probably most of the men I knew were dead. Like the sergeant, I found all this business of dying too much to make sense of – and still do, as I write.

Now that I'm alone, I'd don't know what to do with myself. I should find a shovel and clear the ghastly mess upon the floor. I've thought about doing so more than once and almost got up, only to find I couldn't in the end.

Writing steadies my hand, and my mind too, but I have nothing left to say. When I need them most, I'm shocked to discover that I've emptied myself of words.

Yours,
Fred

2nd July 1916
Emily,

It's evening now, with night not far off. Is it strange to write again in the same day? But then I have no way to send my last letter, and no intention of sending this one. The truth is that I'm not writing to you at all, Emily. These notes are for myself, and have been, I suppose, for a long time... a sad attempt to keep something of myself intact.

Well, it's too late for that now.

I went out an hour ago, looking for a shovel as I'd been planning. It only occurred to me when I got back that I hadn't found one. Instead, I came upon our wounded coming in. Some were borne by the stretcher teams, but most were making their own way. Propped on my crutches, I wandered among them, imagining myself as a ghost amongst ghosts. Altogether we were a ragged and apocalyptic bunch, like drowned sailors trawling the bottom of some ocean.

I've seen hurt men before, and the bodies of the dead, but all of that paled before what I witnessed. It wasn't just the magnitude of the carnage; these injuries seemed so much worse than others I'd come across, even in the hospital. One boy who was hurried past on a stretcher had been shot clean in his face, and there wasn't much left. Yet he was alive, not able to scream because there wasn't enough of his jaw, but staring. Others had lost limbs entirely, or dragged the remnants of half-severed legs and arms. Some of these were amongst the walking wounded, and I might have admired their tenacity if it weren't for the deadness in their eyes: there was too little life in their mechanical hobbling for it to be mistaken as bravery.

Throughout the trench lines they were coming back in their ones and twos, limping or carried or occasionally crawling on hands and knees, like flotsam washing against a ghastly shore. And everything was lit by the reddest, most violent sunset you have ever seen – a bloody, martial orb trying its best to burn through clogging smoke, hanging low over the shattered earth.

I wandered for an hour or so, seeking I knew not what. Perhaps I was hoping for a familiar face. Once I thought I recognised Winters, but the man who turned towards me – cradling one hand, from which had been severed three fingers and a portion of the palm – looked nothing like our sergeant. I muttered a confused apology, but he didn't seem to hear.

Even once I'd set my mind to returning, it took me a while to find my way. The enemy shelling had reordered our trenches, making some impassable and changing the appearance of everything, wiping out landmarks, dislodging signs and turning stretches of duckboard into kindling. Then, when I felt sure I was quite lost and was afraid I'd pass the night exploring those purgatorial channels, I chanced upon a face I knew – though not one I'd hoped to see. A little distance away, sitting upon a slipped mound of sandbags, was the scarred black rat that had invaded my dugout earlier. He was so distinctive that even in the half-light I was certain it was him. He stared at me impertinently and then, with a flick of his whiskers, hopped to the ground and scampered beneath the hem of a gas blanket.

Once I got over my shock, it struck me I must be near my dugout – for rats surely didn't range too far – and then that I recognised the place I'd come to. It was the familiar deep dugout that was reserved for our officers. The impression of light round the blanket told me it was inhabited, and, now that I concentrated, I could hear the faint murmur of conversation. There were men inside, officers who'd either survived the fighting and made it back or else had played their part from the dugout's relative safety.

Confident in my directions, I set out upon my crutches once again. When I finally got back, however, it was to find another familiar face waiting. It was a boy named Tobison who'd come up only recently; quite literally a boy, for I doubt he can have been more than sixteen. When he'd first come to us he'd had a certain sturdiness about him that made his lie of maturity seem more plausible, but the battle had stripped away all that and now, with his tousled hair and wide eyes, he looked more like a child than ever. He had taken a bullet in the side – perhaps more than one, for that entire half of his uniform was drenched in blood. He'd made it as far as my dugout and then evidently seen a comfortable spot and decided to sit down. Perhaps he'd only intended to rest, but I knew he wouldn't be getting up again.

I wondered if there was anything I could do for him. His lips were moving steadily and he seemed aware, but he wasn't saying anything. I thought perhaps his lung had been shot out, for his breath was an awful, congested wheezing. I decided a drink of water might ease his suffering and went inside to fill a cup, but by the time I'd hobbled outside with it his chin was on his chest and the asthmatic whine of his breathing was no more.

I put down my cup of water beside him, like an offering, and went inside once more. I picked my way across the carnage of the floor and sat upon my bunk. I felt nothing; not sadness or pain or anger or even hunger, though I couldn't remember when I'd last eaten. It was as if I'd become immune to all sensation.

After a long time had passed, I became dimly aware of movement, out of the corner of my eye. I moved my head, taking care not to be sudden. I think I knew already what it would be. Sure enough, there was the red rat. He was squatting upon the farther bunk, as though surveying the consequences of his leadership. He didn't seem at all perturbed by the sight of so many rodent dead.

I stood, with infinite slowness. He wasn't watching me. Like the wounded men I'd passed, he didn't seem even aware that I was present.

I knew with terrible clarity what I had to do.

Despite my wound, I've never moved so fast. He tried to scurry away, but in a flash I'd got my hands around him. Once he realised I had him soundly and what I meant to do, he turned on me in a frenzy, clawing and biting at my fingers. I carried him across the room and struck his head with all my strength against the stove, again and again and again. It wasn't long before he stopped fighting me, and not long after that when he went altogether limp. His head by then was a smear across the stove's greenish belly. I tossed his body away, into a dark corner. I didn't want to look at what I'd done.

That was a few minutes ago. I know what I did was right, a necessary act. I know too that my work is incomplete. There were Mills bombs stuffed into Tobison's pockets. I will take a couple. Now that I've slain one rat general, it's only right I should go hunt the other. I'll go into his hole, and bring it down upon both our heads if need be. It's time, at any rate, that all of this was over.

I'll leave this letter here. Perhaps someone will find it, and so it will find you. Perhaps it's better if it never does. I wouldn't have you remember me like this, as a shadow of who I was. When I remember you now I think of our wedding day, and of how very beautiful and bold and sure you were. I hope you'll think of me the same ... for what I was and not what I've become.

Yours, now and forever,
Fred

From: Major Thursby
To: Lt. Col. Allen
4th July 1916
Sir,

Following upon my earlier report of the incident that occurred on the evening of the 2nd July, I am pleased to pass on to you that Capt. Williams is likely to recover from his wounds, which are now being considered as minor. He will be shipped back to England within the week. Capt. Carver, however, died in the night, from severe trauma to the head, making the final death toll four officers – including Major Swift and Captains Tyler and Berry – and two subalterns, Peters and Sourby. I suppose one must also include the perpetrator himself, 2nd Lt Frederick Barrister, whose severely mutilated body has been identified from his tags.

Regarding my earlier concern that 2nd Lt Barrister's actions were in some way a protest, either against a particular officer or the war in general, or part of some wider conspiracy or mutiny, I now believe that this is not the case. I enclose letters from Barrister to his wife, which were found in his bunk. These would imply a severe state of mental agitation, perhaps an extreme incidence of "shell shock" or else a poisoning of the blood as a result of his premature discharge from the clearing station. There is nothing to suggest that Barrister held any grudge, or an ill-feeling towards the British Army; I'm informed, in fact, that until his recent wounding he was considered an exemplar of bravery and good discipline.

As I'm sure you'll agree, these letters cannot be forwarded to his wife, even in censored form, and the whole matter will be best kept a secret. Accordingly, I have put out word to the men that the explosion was the result of shelling. I have also written to the lady in question, advising that 2nd Lt Barrister was killed in action. I trust, sir, that this meets with your approval.

Yours sincerely,
Major Charles Thursby

~

"The War of the Rats", the one previously unpublished story in this collection, came directly out of research for an as yet unreleased novel. Having spent months reading up on the subject of the First World War, I was beginning to feel frustrated by the fact that there was so much I wanted to say that I knew I wouldn't be able to find a place for. Principally, I didn't have an outlet for the anger and revulsion I felt at reading so many tales of lives cut short and disfigured, or for the sheer grotesqueness of much of what I'd come across. It was ideal fare for a horror story, not so much so for a science-fiction novel set largely away from the trenches.

The decision I reached was to pour all that negative feeling into another project, which would end up being "The War of the Rats". While the story is obviously fictitious, it would be a stretch to say that it exaggerates; if anything I got to the end feeling that nothing I could have written would have come close to the worst excesses of reality. As anyone who's done even the most casual investigation into the subject will testify, the horrors of the First World War are nearly beyond comprehension, and certainly beyond overstatement.

Incidentally, the fact that "The War of the Rats" is, at least in part, a love story, is due largely to my primary source material: the memoirs of a young soldier named Harold Chapin, released on Kindle as One Man's War *and a fascinating, heart-breaking read. Harold's diaries were also responsible for my greatest worry, which was that I'd inadvertently end up trivialising my subject. The conclusion I came to was that it would be impossible not to, but also that sometimes that isn't a valid reason not to write about something. As important as it is not to treat lightly the events of one of the most shameful and needlessly brutal conflicts in our species' history, it's every bit as crucial that we keep talking about the First World War in all its horrifying detail.*

The Sign in the Moonlight

You will have heard, no doubt, of the Bergenssen expedition – if only from the manner of its loss. For a short while, that tragedy was deemed significant and remarkable enough to adorn the covers of every major newspaper in the civilised world.

At the time I was in no position to follow such matters. However, in subsequent months I've tracked down many journals from that period. As I write, I can look up at the wall to see a cover of the *New York Times* I've pinned there, dated nineteenth of May 1908, bearing the headline, "Horror in the Himalayas: Bergenssen five reported lost in avalanche."

In a sense, I suppose, it's a spirit of morbidity that draws me back to those days upon the mountain and their awful finale, which I failed to witness only by the purest chance. Equally, there's a macabre humour in the thought that to almost all the world I am dead, my body shattered and frozen in the depths of some crevasse. But what draws me most, I think, is the memory of what I saw after I left Bergenssen and the others – that knowledge which is mine uniquely. It's without disrespect to the *Times* that I say they know nothing, nothing whatsoever, of the horror of Mount Kangchenjunga. Likely, there is no one else alive who does.

No rival can rightly be offended when I say that Bergenssen was the finest mountaineer of his generation. No other but that fierce and hardy Swede would have considered an expedition upon Kangchenjunga after the dramatic failure of the first attempt, and the very suspect circumstances of that failure.

I recollect clearly how we spoke of the matter when he first proposed the climb to me. Coincidence had brought us together in a London gentleman's club that I favoured whenever I was in the city on business. His tone was scathing as he cried, "Aleister Crowley, that self-publicising fool? The man's as much a mountaineer as I am Henry Ford."

"You can't deny that Dr. Jacot-Guillarmod knows his business."

"Pah! I'll deny what I like. I doubt if they ever left Darjeeling."

"Then how do you explain the death of Alexis Pache and those three porters?"

Bergenssen furrowed his brows. "Must I explain it? Perhaps what they say about Crowley is true. Perhaps those unfortunates were sacrificed to whatever ghoulish spirits the man had devoted himself to that week. More likely, he plied Pache with alcohol, drugs, or some yet darker vice and the man remained in India to indulge himself. Even if it's true, a better climber would have known the warning signs of an avalanche and avoided it accordingly."

With retrospect, those words seem bitter with irony, but at the time, I was caught up by the Swede's immense self-confidence and courage, which were as infectious as any cold. "Then you really think it's possible? Freshfield and Sella confirmed the findings of the Great Trigonometric Survey – it truly is the third-highest peak on Earth. It would be a grand achievement."

"I believe there's nothing to be lost in the trying."

"Nothing except our lives."

"Well, of course." He grinned, baring perfectly even white teeth. "So are you with me?"

I was violently tempted to agree on the spot. Instead, I prevaricated, knowing in my heart that I was little more than a hobbyist and, in the final analysis, not fitted to such a venture. Bergenssen's dream was a marvellous one, but outside the smoky environs of the club it would evaporate and, though I might think of our conversation with a certain wistfulness, that would soon pass.

I was wrong. That month brought both personal and business misfortunes and, with each fresh trial, my mind called back to Bergenssen and to misty, snow-clad vistas. By the end of February, almost in despair, I wrote a brief note and mailed it immediately. If the offer still stood, then I was in.

Bergenssen's reply came three weeks later, by telegram to my offices. Aside from the date, time and place for our rendezvous it bore only a simple message: GOOD TO HAVE YOU SIR.

I won't trouble the reader with facts that can be gleaned elsewhere, and which have no bearing upon the substance of my tale. The details of our preparation are common knowledge, and the names of our three companions may be found from many sources, not least the May obituaries.

Bergenssen – somewhat contradicting his earlier comments to me – thought it wise to follow the route established by Crowley and Jacot-Guillarmod, and if we didn't all agree with his logic then there was no question of debate. He was our leader absolutely, and no one would have suggested the excursion become a democracy.

Therefore, after much prevarication on the part of the local authorities, we began in India, and approached our objective via the Singalila Ridge in West Bengal. From Ghum, we trekked through Jorpakri, Tongly, Sandakphu and Falut, in an unremitting downpour of the most torrential rain I've known.

There's little else to tell of those days, except that Bergenssen travelled under something of a funk, which in turn infected the rest of our party, even down to our squadron of porters. He avoided any questions as to what had put him out of sorts, and so I took it for a mood of grim determination, or perhaps mere consequence of the abysmal weather, leaches, and other hardships.

In any case, we made good progress. We proceeded in short order through Gamotang, whence the work of mountaineering began in earnest, and on through successive camps until – late of an afternoon, with violet hints already softening the robust blue of the Himalayan sky – we came upon camp five.

In my mind's eye I'd expected some place remarkable, befitting the violence that had occurred nearby. In fact, it was nondescript, nothing more than a small mound nestled in the shadow of one minor peak. Strangely, this disappointment didn't so much mitigate my sense of nervous excitement as increase it – as though I'd unconsciously decided to seek elsewhere for the tragic drama the scenery failed to provide.

We were all of us very quiet, however, and Bergenssen seemed practically catatonic, having said not a word all through the afternoon. By the time we'd pitched our tents and retired, the sky was a dark and livid purple that made the snow seem almost black, and my excitement had risen nearly to fever pitch – though I still couldn't say why, or what might possibly relieve it.

Rather than settle down to sleep, I sought out Bergenssen, and was pleased to find him in better cheer than he'd been throughout the day. Without to-do, I said, "This is the point where the Crowley expedition floundered, isn't it? Do you think we're in any danger?"

"If Crowley's to be believed then no, none whatsoever. He blamed the matter entirely on Tartarin and Righi's incompetence, as I'm sure you know."

I detected a note in Bergenssen's tone. "And if he *isn't* to be believed?"

"Well... it's all very strange, you know." He lapsed into silence, and for a while it seemed this cryptic statement would be his last word on the matter. Finally, he continued, "One newspaper claimed that he heard their screams but chose to stay in his tent, drinking tea rather than hurrying to their aid. There was a quote I memorised: 'A mountain accident of this sort is one of the things for which I have no sympathy whatever,' he said. Can you believe that?"

"If there's anything in the rumours about him, I can. They refer to him in certain circles as 'the wickedest man in Britain'. Do you really think it's strange that he'd let his fellows go to their deaths unaided?"

"That? No, that isn't it."

There followed another long pause. These silences unsettled me more than anything because they were so out of keeping with Bergenssen's characteristic bluster. What he eventually said, however, was nearly as unexpected. "You know, I suppose, what Kangchenjunga means?"

I'd passed a few hours in research before we set out. "The Five Treasures of Snows... the natives associate the five peaks with the five repositories of their god."

"Did you know that Crowley claimed the porters were willing to continue – the next morning, that is, after the accident? He said they told him that the spirits of the mountain had been propitiated. One death for every peak."

"But every account reports only four deaths, those of Pache and three of the porters."

Bergenssen looked away, to stare distractedly at the wall of the tent. "Yes. I know."

I sensed that his brief spell of loquacity had come to an end. I bid him goodnight and retired to my own small shelter. Feeling suddenly exhausted, I climbed straight into my sleeping bag and extinguished my lamp.

Yet sleep was not forthcoming. As often happens, bodily tiredness served only to exacerbate the activity of my mind. Outside, the wind ranged between eerie soughing and a penetrating, almost feline screech. Every so often, a crash marked the passage of some loose snow bank into the abyss.

As I lay staring into perfect darkness, I thought upon the rumours I'd heard of Aleister Crowley, tales he seemed to delight in and even propagate. I wondered what succour such a man could hope to find amidst the soul-wrenching desolation and wild beauty of the Himalayas. I imagined myself at the very spot where Crowley had sat, listening as his colleagues were torn from the mountain face, sipping tea as they tumbled down and down toward horrific deaths.

I don't remember falling asleep, but I have vague recollections of dreams in which I was led not by the hardy Bergenssen but by Crowley himself, who beckoned me through the most hazardous of routes, paths he crossed effortlessly only to laugh and caper when I couldn't follow with the same ease.

I remember how I raged at him – and how my cries only made him laugh the harder.

I woke late. It was that, I suppose, that saved my life.

I transitioned abruptly from deep sleep into wakefulness, and realised the sounds from outside were my colleagues preparing for our departure. Yet I had no urge at all to move. I felt cold beyond belief, and it was more than I could do to control my shivering. Nevertheless, I struggled into my coat and boots, whilst the urge to vomit rose in my gullet.

The moment I stepped outside, Bergenssen rushed over. "My God, man, are you all right? You look like death! Can you stand?"

I struggled to control my thoughts. "I had the malaria," I said. "Last year, in Egypt. I think perhaps it's back." I brushed a palm across my brow, found it clammy. "I'm afraid I'll be going nowhere today."

"Not to worry, old man," Bergenssen said – though in fact, he looked more dejected even than I felt. "It's a poor time for a delay, though."

I couldn't see how this was true. The wind was high, visibility was poor, and in all it promised to be a bad day for mountaineering. When I pointed this out, he said, "Yes, but we have a while yet. I wanted badly to make camp six."

I was startled by the lack of sympathy in his tone. It was a sort of childish spite that made me say, "You should go on. I'll be better soon, I'm sure." Then, beginning to realise how foolishly I was jeopardising myself, I added, "If you rope the worst parts and send someone back in a day or two, I'll be able to catch up."

Bergenssen nodded vigorously. I could see that he very much wanted to believe me. "Yes, I suppose that's the only way. You can manage, can't you? I'd leave one of the porters, you know..."

"Yes?" I said, with sudden hope.

"But we'll need them all at six, you see."

My heart sank. I felt a flush of horror at the thought that the man before me was nothing like the Bergenssen I knew; that no words I could say would move him. "Don't worry," I told him. "What's the worst that can happen to me here?"

So they set out, and I watched until they disappeared. Had I any premonition? I remember being ill at ease, but of course there was the sudden rush of sickness, my half-remembered nightmares, and Bergenssen's uncharacteristic behaviour. With all that, it was easy to dismiss any doubts as fanciful.

Yet very soon I had graver reasons for concern. The weather worsened drastically: the wind rose in a matter of minutes, until soon it was a gale, flinging pirouettes of snow and wailing banshee-like across the cliffs. It wasn't long before I was driven back into my tent, where I huddled, shivering, hoping against hope to hear the sounds of their return.

What I heard instead was the worst thing I could have expected – a colossal crash that seemed to go on for minutes before it subsided into a low muttering.

It could only be an avalanche.

I think I grew feverish then, if I hadn't been already. I know it wasn't long after the avalanche that I convinced myself my companions would not be returning. They were gone, and I was alone.

I shouted and raved for a while. Afterwards, I imagined I'd returned to lucidity. The truth was that my temporary madness had taken a different turn. I was sure I should go outside and start back to camp four, where a portion of our entourage waited with supplies. If I didn't, I would be buried – as Bergenssen and the others had been buried.

I staggered outside. The storm was like nothing I'd seen. Visibility was non-existent, except when a flash of lightning offered brief and violent illumination. Other than that, there was only darkness and snow, mixed inseparably, an ever-shifting funnel that howled around my every step.

Within a minute I'd lost all trace of my tent. On one level, I realised I was as likely to blunder off a cliff as to come anywhere near our last camp, but that realisation did nothing to slow my steps. Increasingly, I was unsure of where I was going, or why. Was something pursuing me? Yes, that was it – now that I thought, I could hear it, hear its measured steps through the bludgeoning of the gale. Was this a thing or a man? Perhaps it was something of both.

I stumbled often and fell more than once, but I seemed to have grown oblivious to pain, or sense, or anything but my fear. I reeled without direction, with no sense of time, unaware even of the storm.

I don't remember finding the valley. All I recollect is a change in the pitch of the wind, a relaxing in the lash of the snow against my back. It seemed quite abrupt. There was light, for the first time in ages. At first, I thought it was artificial. Then I recognised the pallid glow of the moon. It hung low and gigantic, as though I'd scaled a peak that had somehow brought us face to face. The light was sufficient for me to see the crevasse walls to either side – and ahead, the building that rose where those walls met.

I thought it must be a monastery, but it looked as much like a fortress, with four windowless tiers raised on columns, each level roofed in the peculiarly sharp and steep Tibetan style. The wide doors were of plain, black wood, and there was none of the usual ornamentation, except for one detail – the huge, golden pentagram mounted high upon the fourth storey.

At that sight, though I might rationally have assumed myself rescued and safe, my fear redoubled. I managed one more step, before all the strength left my body at once.

I pitched forward. The blackness took me, and – God help me – I was grateful.

I woke by stages.

For some immeasurable period, I'd been aware of sensations – motion, and later, the cool of water on my brow – but had lacked any understanding of what those feelings meant or how they came to be. I was oblivious to the passage of time. Regardless of whether my eyes were open or closed, they were met by the same ruddy gloom. I was afraid, but in an indistinct way, as one might fear the concept of dying more than the prospect itself. I've no doubt that my fever was still raging, for I remember phases of awful cold and enormous heat.

Eventually, I examined my surroundings with something approaching clarity. I was muddled, the effort of moving my neck made it ache cruelly, and my inner clothes were moist with sweat, but I was lucid enough for curiosity. However, the room I found myself in was very plain. I lay on a low, hard bed, and the only other furnishings were a stool in the opposite corner, a small table beside me, and a narrow brazier. I thought it might be a cell, though there was no indication of a lock on the door. Then I remembered the building I'd seen, and how I'd thought it must be a monastery. The chamber seemed plain enough to be a monk's.

Yet that was strange in itself. If Crowley had been correct then we'd reached to around twenty-five thousand feet; even a conservative estimate placed us at well above twenty-thousand. Such a height was tremendously isolating, too much so for any regular supply or communication from the outside world.

I thought back to the research I'd done before joining with Bergenssen. There'd been one sect in particular who considered Kangchenjunga sacred, and who might very well have built a monastery high amongst its peaks. What were they called? The Kirati, that was it – descendants of an ancient local people, practitioners of a religion rife with shamanism and ancestor-worship. If I remembered rightly, their god was "Tagera Ningwaphuma," called the Supreme Knowledge. Perhaps here, high upon the mountain, I had come upon one of their extreme outposts.

Then I remembered the pentagram above the door. Maybe it wasn't the Kirati after all – or if it was, some even more obscure offshoot cut off from the rest. *Five points*, I thought, *five points for five peaks*, and something in the notion made me shudder.

I climbed unsteadily to my feet. The effort made my head spin, and only a hand outstretched to the wall kept me standing. After a minute, however, the dizziness began to pass. I crossed the stone floor by small steps and tested the door. Sure enough, there was no lock. It swung open freely.

The man who waited outside, who turned at the sound of the door's opening, was swathed in robes of deep crimson. He resembled any other priest of the region, except for two details: his robe was hooded and the hood drawn up, so that I could see only a crude hint of features, and in his hand he gripped a wooden staff which he clearly didn't require for support.

He moved to bar my way. He was smaller than I was, but agile. He said something I didn't understand; it didn't sound like any dialect of Tibetan I'd heard. Something in the words and in his stance made me nervous.

"I'm grateful for your hospitality," I said, "but I won't

impose any further." I don't know if I really expected him to understand English. When he evidently didn't, I added in broken Tibetan something to the effect of, "Now I must go."

He pressed closer, with the staff upraised, as if herding me back into my cell. He spoke again, this time more abruptly.

"No," I said, reverting to English. "My friends... on the mountain..." I'd suddenly thought of Bergenssen, and the previously unconsidered possibility that someone might have survived. "Thank you, I must be leaving."

This time he spoke loudly, and waved one hand close to my face as though swatting at an insect.

Suddenly, I felt terribly afraid. I pushed him away. At that, he looked as though he'd shout along the passage for help. In panic, I grabbed for his staff, and had it away from him before he even realised what was happening. He took a swift step back. I swung clumsily. The blow caught his shoulder. In a crouch, he backed off again, and I knew he was preparing to run. I struck again. This time, he slipped backward and his balance went. His head struck the wall with a ghastly slap.

I stood panting for a while, staring down in uncomprehending horror. Finally, I realised the dark trickle pooling between the cobbles was blood. Was he dead? I dared not check. But he wasn't moving, and I could hear no sound of breathing.

It had been an accident.

Or had it?

In either case, how could I explain?

I'd committed an abominable deed. I had killed a man on the most tenuous of grounds. Yet all I felt was fear, so profound that it swallowed every other sensation or possibility, morality included.

I decided I must hide the body. That might forestall any suspicion until I could get out of there. Setting the staff down, I grasped under his shoulders and, with much clumsy effort, managed to manoeuvre him into the room where I'd awoken.

I tried to drag him onto the bed, but the task proved beyond me. I let him flop to the floor instead. As I did so, his hood fell back, and I finally saw his face. He was slim-featured, quite young, and unexceptional – except for the scar on his cheek.

It was a perfect pentagram of whitened skin.

I shuddered with a feeling far worse than fever. Something was terribly wrong here, and in that moment the fact I'd killed a man didn't seem the worst of it. What had I stumbled onto, high upon Kangchenjunga?

If I were under threat and had no means to reason with my captors, if I was already responsible for the death of one of their number, there could be no question but that I'd be safer even in the tempest outside. I returned to the corridor and considered it properly. It was very plain, and so long that I thought it might stretch the entire length of the building. Spaced along its length were other rooms or cells at roughly even intervals. At the far ends were double doors, each pair like those I'd observed from the outside.

It seemed a safe assumption that one set led out to the valley from whence I'd arrived. But which?

I settled on the nearest. In the interest of covertness, and also because its tip was sodden with blood, I abandoned the staff, choosing to support myself against the wall instead. I moved softly, on the very border of panic, convinced I'd be discovered at any instant.

In fact, I reached the doors without incident. After much nervous hesitation, I pushed one slightly open. Only blackness lay beyond. I pushed harder. Crouched low, I eased through the gap.

I was aware of a large space, then of light at its centre, and finally of figures standing within the illumination. Cockroach-like, I scurried through the shadows, hoping for some intense dark to conceal me. I was sure I'd be seen. Yet when I paused to look, the figures were still absorbed.

That calmed me fractionally – enough that I could take in the scene about me. I crouched at the edge of a large, circular chamber cleanly split into halves. The inner portion, where I knelt, was bordered only by plain stone walls. The other, however, presented a series of arches to the most astonishing vista. Evidently we were perched on the very edge of the mountainside, because the view was horizonless and dizzying.

At the centre of the room, directly above the point where the figures were gathered, a narrow well in the domed ceiling let in a beam of scintillating moonlight. Beneath, borne on a low pedestal, sat a large, pentangular dish of crystalline filigree, so delicate and translucent that it might have been carved from ice. So much did it glow and its surface ripple that the dish seemed to have been filled by the rays shining from on high.

I could make no sense of what I saw, except to find it strange and frightening. Nor had I time to consider. Suddenly the figures, who previously had appeared sunken in reverie, began to mill about and to converse in that clipped tongue the monk had employed. I feared I'd been discovered, and tensed instinctively. But none of them were looking in my direction.

It occurred to me they must be wondering after their missing companion, and this was confirmed when a delegation hurried out through the double doors. A minute later came shouts, and a second party followed the first. For a while, there was much activity. I was sure that at any instant one of them would penetrate the shadows and discover me. Yet, though they had time to scour the place, not one seemed to consider that I might have intruded upon their sanctum. Eventually they reconvened, and I allowed myself the faintest release of held breath.

My relief was premature – and hopelessly misjudged.

The gathering split into two factions. Five of the monks surrounded the pentangular dish, whilst the others retreated to form a crescent round it, with the open side in the direction of the doors. Immediately they set up a chant, in a language just as unfamiliar but quite different from the one they'd employed before.

The words played havoc on my nerves, and brought incomprehensible images into my mind – as though I perceived something I couldn't rationally grasp. As the chant heightened, raising towards crescendo, so the slant of moonlight seemed to brighten, and then to pulse. At last, it was as though a column of brilliant, throbbing whiteness fell through the centre of the room. Though this scorched my eyes, it never occurred to me to look away. The dish seemed full almost to overflowing, as though brimming with fluid light.

The five monks assigned to the pentagonal tips, who so far had played no part, lurched abruptly to life as if galvanised. Each grasped his respective point and heaved with all his might. Slowly, the bowl began to tip.

As impossible as I knew it to be, I expected the contents to run out, to splash like mercury over the floor. Instead, just as impossibly, they were projected – in a manner that bore no resemblance to the projection of light. The flow seemed to crawl and seethe through the air. It fell upon the door, where it splashed like thrown paint.

When it settled, a glimmering pentagram hung upon the boards.

I'd barely registered all this when the chant adopted a new tone, shifting register without any loss of intensity. My attention was focused entirely on the doors. They looked soft and unreal under the stamp of fluid moonlight.

They seemed to shudder – once, twice, and a third, most violent, time.

With a force that made wood shiver like paper, they sprang open.

I fell backwards. I think I even cried out. If I did, the sound drew no attention. All thought was devoted to that hideous mantra – which seemed now like a wail of condensed experience, of horrible knowing borne by unfathomable words.

All eyes hung on the open doorway.

I couldn't help but look.

My first thought was of a mirror, so similar was the scene beyond. There was the circular chamber, there the arches opening onto inconceivable space, the pedestal, the figures clustered about it.

Yet almost straight away I perceived a difference. The view through the distant arcade was not the one behind me. Those stark grey pinnacles were unlike any on Earth.

Then it struck me. They weren't of Earth at all.

If they were, what could explain the blue-green orb hung in the sky behind? I knew with absolute certainty that I looked upon a world not my own. More, I felt sure it was our moon, the very same that cast its rays through the ceiling – whose radiation had somehow riven a path through untraversable space.

But if that was true, who were those unshapely forms, robed like their earthly brethren, who turned towards us? They were not men; too tall, too long in limb. A faint and bluish glow ebbed from within their cowls. As they moved towards the door, the shadows flickered jarringly around them. The swish of an arm revealed... what? Not a hand.

They lurched closer, and my heart contracted. I knew that something wholly, inimically inhuman approached. They were almost upon the doorway, and I was frozen. I could only watch – as the foremost reached the brink, tilted its head, as I caught a glimpse of what lay beneath that updrawn hood...

With a cry of horror, I threw myself forward. All I could think to do was hurl myself upon the pentangular dish. I struck it with all my strength. It moved a little, and the moonbeam wavered.

Every one of the creatures turned its stare upon me. Together, they hissed in fury.

I heaved. I thought my bones would break before that dish moved, and still I drove against it. For something so seemingly light, it felt like lead set in concrete. I pushed, without hope, too desperately afraid to stop. At any moment, one of the monks – or, unimaginably worse, one of the moon-beings – would pry me away. I pushed harder, though I thought my tendons must snap. When finally the dish shifted, it was by hardly an inch. I could do no more; I fell back, panting, my back and arms slick with sweat. I'd given my all, and still I'd failed.

Yet somehow, that minute jilt was enough. Free of its axis, the dish tilted, rocked – and fell.

Shattering, it was like ice cascading across the cobbled floor.

Looking back to the entrance, I saw the doors still stood open – but upon that familiar passage I'd arrived by. I sank to my knees, no longer concerned for my safety. Let the monks tear me to pieces if they would. I'd saved my world from something appalling. Even in death, I could take comfort in that.

No hand fell. No blow was struck.

When I eventually dared look up, I understood why. Dust was showering from the ceiling, as though the building were in the grip of a minor earth tremor. An instant later, I felt it, a pulse travelling up through the floor tiles. The pulse became an unrhythmic throb. A block tore loose from the roof and shattered, showering us in fragments. One of the monks screamed and stumbled.

Though I hardly glanced back, I'm sure I was the only one who tried to flee. The monks merely stood, resigned, as their blasphemous temple ruptured around them. Only I ran – darting amongst the falling rubble, certain that at any instant I'd be pulverised. I forgot my weakened state, forgot everything except the hope of night air on my face.

Reaching the second set of double doors, I found them already mangled and half off their hinges. I pressed through the gap this afforded, and still I didn't stop. I kept going until the last rumbling subsided – until the night was utterly still. Only then did I pause to look back.

There was nothing to see but a vast bank of snow, pierced here and there with hints of shattered masonry.

The monastery had been utterly erased.

You may wonder how I survived to write this record.

I wonder too. I walked, or staggered rather, for some time – hours, days, I can't say. I don't remember how I discovered the remnants of camp four. I came to myself huddled in a tent, with only fragmentary recollections of the intervening time.

I suppose I'd been uncommonly lucky. What had happened, I later discovered, was this: five men died that day on the way to camp six – Bergenssen, our three mountaineering companions, and one of the Sherpas. The rest of the porters turned back immediately, found me gone from camp five and so backtracked to four. Meeting with the party stationed there, they had democratically decided to forget the whole sorry mess and return home. From either idleness or some vestigial loyalty, they'd left both the tents and the supplies.

Thus I found shelter, food, and medicine enough to nurse myself back to health. In the end I felt capable of attempting the downward climb. It was slow progress, but I was in no hurry. In Sandakphu, I learned the truth regarding Bergenssen and the others. It came as no surprise. I carried on, deeper into India. I had some money with me, and access to more. I felt dimly that I could not go home.

I write now from a location I choose not to disclose. I will send this tale to a number of reputable journals, in the hope that one may see fit to print it, whether they believe it or no.

No one should think to seek me out. They won't find me. I've come to realise I have too many unanswered questions weighing on my mind. What had been that impossible passage in the moonlight? What those gangling, unearthly figures? The monastery had been destroyed, its tenants crushed and buried; yet dare I hope that there were no other temples, no other routes between worlds, no acolytes so destitute in soul that they might open them?

And thinking upon that last, one more inescapable question came to my mind: what part in this monstrous affair was played by Aleister Crowley, so-called "wickedest man in Britain." Could that wickedness extend to the betrayal of all mankind to something malicious and inhuman?

I have my suspicions.

Now, too, I have a little knowledge; hints to dark and sordid truths, the corrupted fruits of my research. In the course of my search, I have made allies... a very few. The one thing I lack now is proof. When the time should come that I have it, only then will I return – and there shall be a reckoning for the horrors of Kangchenjunga.

~

Finally, the title story! Though – a small confession – it wasn't always intended to be. That honour was originally meant to go to "The War of the Rats", as the longest and newest work. But since Duncan, who had by this point produced interior illustrations for every story in the collection, couldn't get the picture for that particular tale to a point he felt was cover-worthy, we eventually agreed to go instead with one he'd already produced an absolutely stunning image for. It turned out to be a decision that felt right as soon as we'd made it, and now it's impossible to imagine anything else on the front of this book.

In fact, I'll go further: I don't know that any tale in the collection sums up its spirit quite as perfectly as "The Sign in the Moonlight". It's absolutely a weird tale, one that might even have freaked out Lovecraft himself a little, what with his notorious phobia of the cold. It certainly creeped me out as I was writing it. It was genuinely strange how this story came together, and how much my research threw up real life details that fit perfectly, not only with the narrative I was constructing but with each other. A lot of that research went into "Sign", quoted almost directly; the anecdote regarding Crowley's reaction to the death of his mountaineering companions is factual, for example, and came, if I remember rightly, from Crowley's own diaries. The details about Kangchenjunga are also largely true.

All told, I've never before or since written something that so seemed to be taking on a life of its own. As far as I'm concerned, that makes "The Sign in the Moonlight" a legitimately weird weird tale, which is just one more reason why it's the perfect title story for this collection.

My Friend Fishfinger by Daisy, Aged 7

Fishfinger is my bestest friend in the whole world. And she says I'm her bestest friend too, even though she doesn't have any other friends, but I'm still the best anyway so that's okay.

Her name isn't really Fishfinger, that's just what everybody at school calls her, because they say she smells like fish and she looks a bit like a fish as well. And she does too but I still like her and anyway they all smell too so there. My mommy says it's mean and I should call her by her proper name but Fishfinger says she doesn't mind. She does when other kids call her it because they're mean and they don't like her but I'm nice she says and I'm her bestest friend so it's okay. But really her real name is Samantha.

Fishfinger hasn't lived in my town very long, her and her mom and her dad, who I call them Mr and Mrs Fishfinger but that's not really their names but I can't spell their real names, they used to live in another town near the sea and that was called Innsmouth. Fishfinger says it was nice there and no one was mean to her at her old school because she wasn't different there, and nobody said she smelled like fish, and but then they had to move but she doesn't know why they did.

Fishfinger and her mom and her dad don't ever come to church with us, so I asked her one time, did that mean that she doesn't believe in the baby Jesus like how we do? And she said, no, they have their own God who's different from ours and he isn't called God his name is D-A-G-O-N, that's how she spelled it. And he gives them gold and all sorts of things she said. And I asked why she doesn't go to a special church so that she can pray and sing songs and she said they can't because their God lives in the sea and they had a church at home only it wasn't called a church but they can't have one here because there's no sea.

I thought that was silly, but my teacher says you shouldn't laugh at people because their religion is different from yours, even when it is silly.

Fishfinger's mom seems nice even though she doesn't say much but I don't like Fishfinger's dad because he looks at me strange like how people look when they're hungry. And one time I saw his neck and he had like what my goldfish his name was Goldie what my goldfish had for breathing, they are called gills. I thought he had those and I told my mom and she said that was silly because people don't have gills only fishes do. But every other time he was wearing a big jumper and so I couldn't see his neck and my mom said it was a dream maybe or I made it up but I didn't but maybe it was a dream. I've had lots of funny dreams lately. One dream I had there was a big fish man, he was as tall as ten houses on top of each other and he wanted to eat me but then I woke up and it was only a dream. And they can't hurt you my mom said but they can still be scary I said.

Anyway, I don't like Fishfinger's dad much at all. One day he asked me a funny question, he said, are you a virgin and I said that I didn't know what one of those is except that the Virgin Mary was one and he said well if I didn't know then I was. And Fishfinger's mom said of course she is, don't go asking her things like that, you'll upset the girl she's only eight (but I'm not I'm seven) and he told me he was very sorry and he hoped I wasn't upset and I said it was okay but I still don't like him.

Only I do like him a little bit because him and Mrs Fishfinger said that I can go on vacation with them if I like. They said, would I like to come and be a little friend for Samantha (that's Fishfinger her real name) to play with. And I said that would be lovely because me and mom and dad aren't going on holiday this year, last year and the year before that we went to stay with grandma and granddad but we can't this year because grandma is poorly and her legs are gone funny.

And so me and Fishfinger are going to go to Innsmouth which is where she lived before she lived here and she's going to show me all her favourite places and her old school and all sorts of things.

And Mr Fishfinger says that he will take me to the specialist place there is but it's a secret so I can't tell anybody but I can write it down that's okay. It's a big rock in the sea and they do their religion there it's like how in our church there's the high up place where the vicar stands only they have a big rock instead and that's better he says because then their God can come and talk to them properly. He's a very hungry God, Mr Fishfinger says, and if I'm extra especially good then maybe they'll let me feed him. One time we went to the zoo and I fed the sea lions and they clapped their hands and did a dance. It'll be just like that except better.

I am looking forward to it lots and lots and lots.

~

"My Friend Fishfinger by Daisy Aged 7" was written with little forethought and in one mad spree. I received one of my nicest ever reviews for this story, which acknowledged just how difficult it is for a grown man to write in the style of a seven year old girl. Yet the truth is that it wasn't difficult at all! I don't often talk about characters finding their own voices, but Daisy certainly did, and she went on to more or less write her own story, which required little redrafting and which I'm still entirely happy with nigh on a decade later.

In retrospect, as much as it's basically a rather mean-spirited joke, there was also a little serious intent underlying this one, and it ties into many of the ideas I've come to recognise in my writing. I love pulp fiction, but I can never resist trying to rationalise it. How would real people behave in this situation? Accepting that people are never simply evil – or at least never think of themselves in such terms – how do they rationalise the acts they commit? And Lovecraft's "The Shadow Over Innsmouth", which of course "My Friend Fishfinger" references so heavily, is unusually ripe for such questions. After all, you don't have to tip it too far before it becomes the tragic tale of a dirt-poor community abandoned by its government and its own greedy authorities and driven to increasingly desperate measures. Thus, the beginning of "My Friend Fishfinger" was me seriously wondering just where the good folks of Innsmouth would find all those sacrifices, and what exactly the residents of nearby towns made of their curious neighbours. There's probably a serious tale to be written around such questions – in fact, I'm currently attempting it as a graphic novel – but, unfortunately for poor Daisy, this didn't end up being that story.

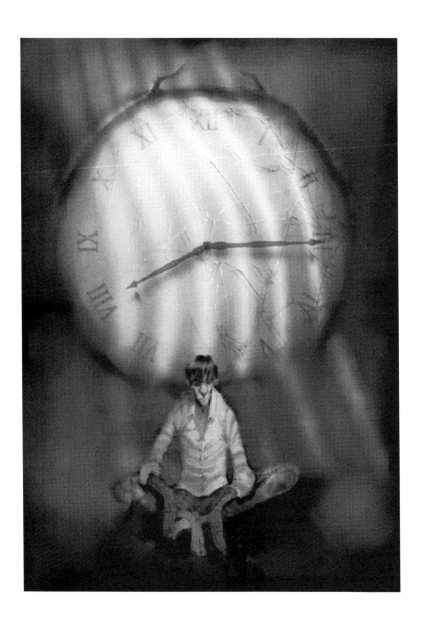

Prisoner of Peace

Today is a day of darkness.

For all that, I can see every brick in the wall, and every crack in every brick. I think somehow that if I only looked hard enough, I could even see into those cracks, and scrutinize their furthest depths.

I know today what's behind me, lying on my sleeping mat. I wish I didn't, but I do.

I tried to scream at first, but no sound came out.

Now, I sit and wait. Forgetfulness will come.

It has to.

Today is a day of darkness.

I've been trying to remember, but it is difficult. More than difficult – it is a trial beyond all reason.

I concentrate, as well as I can. Even then, my memories are like the broken pieces of a pot. Some are missing, some are warped, and the overall pattern is unclear. To release a shard of memory, even for a moment, is to lose it.

Some memories are sharp, and it pains me to hold them. Their loss is a relief, and I hope it will be for good. Some, I know, are valuable, but just as hard to keep.

My name... it is a hard thing to be without a name.

Most of the time it is dark outside my window. When it's dark, I can still see a little, as though everything has been painted with ink of the deepest blue.

Not that there is much to see in my small room. Opposite the door and to the right is a bucket, meant to serve as a toilet. Opposite the door and to the left is a sleeping mat, with two ragged blankets curled at its foot. Between bucket and mat is the window itself, high up, almost against the ceiling.

I sit or stand, with the door to my right and the window to my left. I do this because there is something on my sleeping mat. I know I mustn't ever look at it. However much else I forget, this memory remains. *Do not turn around. Don't look behind.*

Sometimes it is light outside, but the light is far too bright, no easier to see by than the darkness.

I've learned to prefer the darkness to the light.

There is a tapping coming from the next room.

I call it a room, but I know it is a cell – just as I know that my room is a cell. The tapping is irregular, arrhythmic, and I think it is the sound of someone trying to communicate. A pipe runs along the bottom of my wall. If I were to strike it, just so, with the heel of a sandal or a stone perhaps, it would make a noise like the one from the next room.

But I have no sandal, no stone, nothing to rap against the pipe. Nor do I know what the noises mean, if they mean anything at all. If the tapping is a message, it is one I cannot understand, can't reciprocate.

I realise now that I have heard the noise before – and, sometimes, other noises too. On occasions, there is a sound of heavy, booted footsteps. They approach from the near distance, pass my door, continue a little way and then return, recede, approach again.

It can only be someone patrolling the corridor, and I think sometimes to call out. There are many things I could say, many questions I could ask. The footsteps remind me that there was a time when food was left. A bowl placed inside my door and, later, removed. There was rice, always, and less commonly, thin vegetable stew, a little fish.

It seems a very long time since I tasted any of these things.

Perhaps this is why I never call out. Perhaps it is why

the sounds from the neighbouring cell fill me with nothing but unease. What frightens me – more than tapping or the echo of pacing footsteps – is the thought of the answers I might receive.

Sometimes I remember certain things very clearly. Today, it is parts of my past. Not all, not where I was born or how I grew up, not my parents' names or faces. I still don't recall my own name. But I do know how I came to be here.

There was a war, and we were not winning.

News had been scarce. What we heard, we could hardly believe. When you were alone at night, with no soldiers around, no one you asked would tell you any more that the war could be won. All that lay between us and the ignominy of defeat was time, and life had grown so hard that it was difficult to imagine losing could be any worse.

I lived in a shack close to the river. I shared it with a woman. A wife? A sister? I don't know. But I remember with great and almost physical clarity that we were starving. There was no work, and no money to be made if there had been, and even money could not have produced much food in our famished city.

Still, there were those who did not go without quite as we did, whose deprivations were less. In desperation, I stole from one of these. Having no experience in such things, I did so clumsily, and was caught. Soldiers were called for. I thought they would shoot me there and then, and leave my body in the street so that at least the dogs might eat. I was hungry enough by then that the prospect was almost a relief.

The soldiers did not kill me. They took me, instead, to a low concrete building near the centre of the city, and to a cell in the basement of that building.

In this, I suppose, they were merciful. I suppose that is what passes for mercy in such times. Or perhaps my imprisonment was only meant to be temporary, a stay of execution. I briefly entertain the notion that they might yet come for me, might drag me out to face a belated punishment. I know, without knowing how, that this will never happen. Though I have many things to fear, the soldiers are no longer one of them.

It is terrible to think that the promise of a bullet could have been so tempting, terrible to imagine I would have so longed to abandon the woman waiting in that dilapidated riverside shack. Ungratefully, I discover that I despise these memories. I find myself hoping to forget them again soon.

Has this happened before? How many times have I dredged up the past, only to let – or make – myself forget?

Today I am very afraid.

I'm in a room, alone. Everything is in darkness. Though night shows at the bars high in the wall, that alone can't explain this heavy, laden gloom. It isn't just the absence of light but a thickening of the shadows, as though the very air were unclean.

I know I mustn't look behind me – but not what horror I expect to find there if I did. Not daring to turn around, I only sit, quite still in the clotted blackness, staring at the wall.

From beyond the bricks comes a tapping, muffled and irregular. The tapping terrifies me almost as much as the thought of what awaits over my shoulder. I long to cover my ears. What keeps me from doing so is the surety that I would still hear that noise. Just as if I were to look behind me with my eyes closed, I would still see. If it were so easy to escape these horrors, wouldn't I have done so long ago?

I wish I could remember why I'm here – or anything. Even my name eludes me. The bars in the window make me think that I'm being punished. For what? By whom? Surely, every punishment, however deserved, should make at least some measure of sense to the punished. Surely, every sentence must have an end, even if that end were only death.

Perhaps forgetfulness is my only grace. For I must have

done truly terrible things to be here.

Today, there is light outside my window. It has painted my room so brilliantly white that I can no longer make out the bricks in the wall or the shape of the door – and still it builds. I feel the pressure of it against my back, and inside the walls of my skull. I think that if I turned my head even slightly, my eyes would set afire.

The light makes a sound so loud that I can't hear it.

I think this has happened before.

I remember someone unlocking my door.

How could I have forgotten such a thing? Yet I did – and even now, I recollect it only as a distraction, for at the time it didn't seem important. Events far more pressing occupied my attention: a white light, a great darkness – and pain.

His footsteps travelled slowly, haltingly. Not the steady march I've heard since, but the sound a man might make if he moved with difficulty, or perhaps if he were unsure as to the rightness of his actions. I heard him as though at a great distance, for somebody nearby was screaming.

I think it may have been me.

Now I wonder – could I leave this room? What has kept me prisoner all this time? I can't believe it was only ever a closed door.

In this moment, it seems to be nothing except my own fear. I'm afraid of the darkness, of the noises, of whatever lies contorted on my sleeping mat. But I've been afraid of these things for a very long time, and at least they are familiar.

I sit now with the door before me. This puts my sleeping mat and the crumpled shape upon my sleeping mat in the very corner of my eye. It can't be helped. When forgetfulness comes, it may be that the door will remind me.

I despise my cowardice. But who can say if cowardice is

truly a weakness, or all that protects me? Ignorant of everything, even of myself, what can I do except trust to fate?

Today is a day of darkness.

I'm in a room, alone. In the corner of my eye, I see the edge of something, the horizon of a broken shape. I know I mustn't look at it. I think perhaps it would burn my eyes out if I did.

Or something worse. I don't remember. Lacking memory, I hold onto knowledge, however inexplicable. I must not turn my head and look to see what lies on my sleeping mat.

I sit still, confined by what I know but dare not consider, and look only ahead. In front of me is a wooden door. I've been staring at it for what seems an age. Just now, it occurred to me that although this door should be locked, it isn't. There must be reasons why I've stayed in this room when I'm not constrained to do so. But I don't know what they are, and I'm afraid of the thing beside me. What out there could possibly be worse?

I hardly have to touch the door before it swings open. Its hinges make no complaint.

The corridor beyond is exactly as I remember, (as I find that I do remember), exactly as it was when they brought me here. However, there is no guard now as there was then. I wonder what could have called him away, what duty could be more important than this.

I pause, sparing a moment to look through the grille in the door beside mine, without quite knowing why. Only as I do so do I notice the steady tapping from within – though I realise now that it's been there all along, just waiting to be heard.

In the far corner, a figure is crouched. He raps upon the pipe running there, with a sandal or perhaps a stone, or maybe just his own bare, bloodied knuckles. I can't see, for his form is a deeper darkness cut into the gloom, like the mouth of a well at night.

Part of me is afraid. Another part wishes I could tell him how no one will ever answer his patient message. Knowing he would not hear, that if he heard he could not understand, I turn away instead.

I climb the stairs at the far end of the corridor. They are concrete, like the walls, and moisture-stained to green in places. Everything is as it was before: the rooms and corridors I pass through, an office of cheap wood tables, filing cabinets, great teetering piles of paper, and beyond its double doors the street I was once marched through, all of it unchanged – just as I left it, days or months or lifetimes ago.

No, not quite. Now, I am alone. In all of this great city, I think, I'm alone.

It's only as I realise this, the magnitude of my aloneness, that I see the other Hiroshima.

It exists beside or in or through the city I remember. If I see one, the other rolls apart like smoke, and then I tilt my head and it heaves back into focus. Together they fit like the slides of a film played slowly, a flicker of light and dark, opposites not only joined but a single thing. I know this to be true, though I can hardly believe it. Only the barest clues of topography and fractured shells of buildings lead me to believe that this other city could be the place I knew.

Mostly, there is rubble. The wooden buildings – and most of the buildings, like my own small shack, were wooden – are all in pieces, ground together and scattered and jumbled. Amidst this ocean of ruin, relics lie like sea wrack, or else protrude obscenely: a tree, stripped of its branches; a fire truck, charred and skeletal; a torii gate, standing crookedly upon one blackened leg.

Only the sturdiest buildings, like that behind me, have survived in any form. On one, a stubby clock tower, its corner sheared away entirely, points indignantly at an ashen sky. Miraculously, its clock is intact – though no longer working.

It reads eight fifteen. Therefore, it will read eight fifteen forever.

Behind me I see, very clear upon the wall, the silhouette of a man. I think he was a soldier, for I can see his rifle: he holds it up in front of his face as if it will protect him. Since it did not, he will remain like that, a frozen ghost, a shadow without light, in a city where time itself has burned to ashes.

I don't think he's the only one.

There is nothing left for me here, or for anyone. There is only peace, a peace beyond death. I make my way back inside. Now, the filing cabinets are contorted, the desks shattered, the stacks of paper painted as soot across walls and ceiling. I descend the stairs and walk to the last cell on the right, which is mine.

I spare one brief glance for the figure that lies knotted on my sleeping mat. Pain has twisted him into a shape more insect than human. He lies with his face away from me, and the side I can see is cracked and blackened, like earth after a drought.

I turn away. He is nothing but a shell now, and I can't go back.

The concrete, damp and cold, is familiar beneath my knees as I resume my place. The wall is familiar. The darkness is familiar. My fear is a hand that holds me tight.

I shall sit here and try to forget.

Today is a day of light.

The light makes a sound too loud to hear.

I think this has happened before.

~

Perhaps I shouldn't say this, but I will anyway: "Prisoner of Peace" is my favourite of all the horror stories I've written.

The reason for that is that is partly that it falls most closely in line with my own tastes in horror. Ever since I played the video game Silent Hill 2, *for me one of the masterpieces of the genre in any medium, I'd been wanting to try and replicate what I'd found so effective there: the combination of overt violence and grotesqueness with psychological subtexts and the studied build-up of an almost instinctive sense of dread. The impulse to try and incorporate that into a horror story had been with me for a while, but I could never found the right project for it, and I certainly didn't want to end up with a pastiche. Nor was I particularly inclined towards the blood-and-guts side of things, it was definitely more the puzzle box aspect that appealed: the notion of a story in which the external trappings only make sense once you've come to appreciate the character's interior world.*

I don't know how much those Silent Hill *genes show through in "Prisoner of Peace". It's a more subdued affair, melancholy rather than horrifying, not even really intended to be frightening or disgusting but just to try and creep inside the head and scratch away there. It deals in tragedies both individual and societal, and the ultimate horror it finds is all too real; one that's always haunted me as a nadir of what we as a species are capable of.*

On that note, I should probably admit that my account of the atomic bomb-destroyed Hiroshima is inaccurate. At least one of the details mentioned is drawn instead from Nagasaki. That bit of poetic license was a difficult decision to justify to myself, and the reason I ultimately went for the solution I chose was pathetically simple: as anyone who's spent any time looking at pictures of the devastation wrought by a nuclear explosion will know, there simply wasn't a lot left of Hiroshima to describe.

The Door Beyond the Water

The message came to him in dreams, before the second moon of the season: *A man comes to free the imprisoned one.* Nothing more than that.

But for Cha Né – who was shaman, who saw beneath the mystery of things – that sentence was enough to darken his heart with fear such as he'd never known.

The next night he confronted his spirit-guide with the inevitable questions. "Who is this man who comes? Is he of the mountain people? Is he from the hollow tribe?" It hardly seemed possible, unless the ancient truces had been somehow corrupted. "I must know, Shanoctoc."

The feathered guide had hesitated long before answering. "He is Montague Evans. He is not of the three tribes, nor of the lands between the water and the mountains. He is a white man, of the tribe of Henry Johnson. He will arrive before the third moon."

Then Cha Né's guide, his one companion in the Otherworld, sank into the waters of the lake – was swallowed amidst shivering liquid tendrils.

Cha Né knew, without knowing how, that it was the last time they would ever meet.

Day 24

This morning finds us high upon the first incline to the plateau, and so perhaps a day's hike from its summit, certainly no more than two. It's hard to say more certainly, for Johnson's account becomes increasingly erratic around this point, and his comments upon matters of time unreliable. However, we have the map appended to his diaries and the corroboration of the guides. They tell me we draw near to the lands of the Lam, whose territory comprises the whole of the summit region.

Will the Lam prove peaceable? The guides claim so, but they are less than trustworthy themselves of late. They appear nervous, more so the further we ascend. I worry that soon I may no longer be able to rely on their advice.

That concern might be easier to bear if I weren't already ill at ease myself. Undoubtedly the blame lies in my reading and rereading of Johnson's account. It's a task I'd eagerly give up, were it not for the fact that in his lucid moments he made insights that I'd hate to be without. Unfortunately, those moments of clarity grow scarcer the further I read. More and more, the valuable detail of the day's journey is outweighed by description of his nights, and of his dreams – and the narration of those dreams becomes more outlandish with each page. I have no doubt that by this stage in his expedition he was almost lost to the dementia that would soon ravage his mind entirely.

I often think back to that time when I first became properly aware of Johnson. For months, I'd been hunting a means to corroborate my theories regarding the diffusion of myth in regions cut off from outside influence. I'd heard the rumours that still occasionally circulated: the wild-seeming tales of the ethnographer's last, disastrous excursion. I knew of his earlier notoriety, his controversial and often bizarre essays. But he had been forgotten for the most part, or was remembered only in hushed tones.

That merely added to my growing curiosity. The freakish legends surrounding Johnson began to fascinate me, as much if not more than the remarkable similarities between our ideas. However, it was chance rather than diligence that brought me to the accounts of his last expedition, for I hadn't so much as guessed at their existence before I found them mouldering in the depths of the library. It didn't take me long to realise that the lands he'd investigated would be perfect for my own fieldwork, or – despite the protestations of certain faculty members – to organize a trip upon his established route.

Often, too, I find myself remembering my visit to him, after a long day's journey by train. Even in the asylum, Johnson was kept apart. His mania, they said, disturbed the other patients. I recall the expression on his face, how, despite the excruciating brightness of the electric light, he seemed lost in darkness. More, I remember his screams. "Astasoth! Astasoth!" He repeated the meaningless word endlessly.

With memories such as these, accompanied by Johnson's alarming journals, what wonder is it that my thoughts are unsettled? Is it so strange that I should be troubled by nightmares myself?

Cha Né never questioned his responsibility. He was shaman of the Shanopei. Thus, he was guardian of the gate. Neither the mountain people nor the hollow tribe had a shaman, for there could only be one guardian, and always he came of the Shanopei.

Within the lake tribe, the only other was his novice, Cha Poc. Cha Poc was barely more than a child. The boy would not be ready for many years, for – by nature weak of body like all prospective shamans – he was still ravaged by sickness after each journey through dreams. At present, he lay in the adjoining hut, which Cha Né had built upon his arrival. The boy burned with fever, drifting between this world and the other.

Under any other circumstances, Cha Né would have said that if Cha Poc should die then that was as it must be. Another would be found to take the boy's place, for the tribe had never been without a shaman. In the meantime, he would stand alone until another took his own place.

Yet now, Cha Né found himself wishing the boy was older, that he was stronger – that he could be relied upon.

It was a weak and unworthy thought. It was the surest measure of his fear.

Day 26

We achieved the rim of the plateau late this morning, after hours of exhausting climb. However, this small victory has presented fresh difficulties, for our guides have left us, as they threatened they would. They've started back toward their village on the western shore, where Harley and our base-camp await. God only knows what Harley will imagine when they return without us.

Their last comment still rings in my ears: *Death dwells beyond the lake*, or something to that effect. I choose not to guess at their meaning.

There's no doubt we grow close to where the Johnson expedition was routed. Halfway toward the further edge of the plateau, Middleton was forced to take over after Johnson's undeniable breakdown. There followed a further eight days of hasty retreat back to the sea. Through it all, Johnson raved of some being seen only by himself that dogged their steps. Under that intensely morbid influence, Middleton too began to lose his grasp on sanity. When the expedition finally reached their shore encampment, to be reunited with the two members of their party who'd stayed to maintain it, they were all six in a state of uncontrollable mania.

Not one of them ever elaborated on what had happened, and Johnson and Middleton were quite incapable. What details I now know are the composite of three sources: Johnson's original journals; hurried accounts penned by Middleton before his own breakdown; and some barely meaningful notes scrawled by the last of the party to succumb. All of these texts I have with me now.

I wouldn't wish to exaggerate the similarity of my

nightmares to those detailed so intensely by Johnson. I've read his descriptions countless times and been undeniably affected by them. It's unsurprising that they should haunt my rest as they do my waking hours. This is the only reasonable explanation.

I do find it curious, however, that it isn't the more outlandish details that disturb me, from the period when Johnson was unquestionably deranged, but those earlier incidents he narrated with some measure of sanity. Yet perhaps even this isn't really so strange. Henry Johnson was a dreamer, with an appetite for the most bizarre aspects of the cultures he studied. In this, he was very much an anthropologist of the old school.

I believe myself a more rational man than Johnson, and of stronger mind. Thus, I can sympathize with his writings where they remain within the boundaries of the sane. Beyond that point, they can only appal me.

Henry Johnson had been a dreamer. Not by nature an evil man, he had nevertheless fallen easily into the service of the being beyond the gate.

Cha Né had no choice but to battle with Johnson in the Blind Lands. Afterwards, he had defiled Johnson's mind to its very core, and then – for long days and longer nights – had pursued him through nightmares, hunting and destroying any last snatches of reason.

Cha Né had taken no pleasure in this profanation of his role as shaman. Nor could he deny its necessity. He had intended Henry Johnson's madness to serve as warning so that others would not follow. He had done the unthinkable to protect the tribes under his care from an indescribable fate. He would do the same again.

For all that, Cha Né knew now that he had failed.

He had observed the progress of this new intruder from his perch upon the Sun-drenched Cliffs. Montague Evans had reached the Plains of Frozen Light, guided by cloying words of promise from behind the Endless Gate. In this world, the invented world, he could be no more than two days from the mundane shadow of the Gate. Then, in dreams, he would also reach its true form.

Already there were signs that he was succumbing to the ruinous thing waiting for him. Already the battle seemed half lost.

For it was something more and less than a man he'd seen there, staring back from the far cliffs. Montague Evans' dream-self was changing.

Day 27

Last night, in my dreams, I looked out over a vast plain. Great, mottled cysts rose from its surface, which otherwise was glassy and radiant. Amongst these curious mounds, crystalline towers reached into colourless skies. Those edifices were carved in perfect yet nonsensical angles, as if manufactured according to some altogether inhuman geometry. Their upper levels were pitted by what I told myself must have been windows, though I could see no other means of ingress.

In my reverie, I imagined a voice. I knew it was in my mind – but that it wasn't *only* in my mind. Nor were there really words as such, rather a current of sound that somehow held meaning. I can't even truly say that I heard it. For I had no sense of either mind or body, and such terms do little justice to what I felt myself to be. In waking, I find it all but impossible to explain. Our language is hopelessly ill-suited for such things.

I spent an indeterminate time crossing that plain, just as, in reality, we'd traversed the plateau of the Lam through the day. Other than the voice, there was no sound, no sign of any presence. The surface beneath me was adamantine. There was no sun in the sky, no stars. I progressed at a steady pace, moving as if through the exercise of will.

Eventually, with no clear sense of time having passed, I came to the edge of the mesa. So far, my experience had been not wholly unpleasant, at worst like the queasiness that accompanies the first decline into real drunkenness. Now, abruptly, it veered toward the nightmarish.

Before me, a great sinkhole interrupted the landmass on which I stood. Upon its far side, a sequence of steps joined the higher and lower levels – or what appeared to be steps, for their excruciating size meant that no man could have used them so. At the crater's base swam a fluid of rainbow colour, which swirled with unreasonable currents and eddies. All around the basin, cliffs of an opalescent substance ran, shining brilliantly.

None of those details were frightful. Indeed, the liquid and the cliffs surrounding it were startling and splendid. No, the object that filled me with fear – and much worse, with recognition – stood at the base of that distant, gigantic stairway. At the point where it met the luminous waters of the lake, two columns reared. They were of black rock, polished yet unreflective, seeming almost to absorb the light. Hieroglyphs engraved the twin obelisks from base to tip. I couldn't read them, nor even identify them, yet they filled me with dread.

Even the columns, however, awful in their way, weren't the true source of my terror. Rather, it was what lay within them. Another kind of blackness spread between the pillars of black rock. It wasn't simply an absence of light, or that there was nothing there. Instead, there stretched an endless void – not the lack of space but its absolute reflection.

And there was worse, even than that. The voice in my head, the not-sound I'd unquestioningly followed – it issued from that impossible dimension. Its meaning, now, was almost clear. I knew the voice had led me here, and for a reason.

I was helpless. Whatever purpose I'd been summoned

for, I would certainly have played my part – had I been alone.

The realisation crept upon me slowly. I was being watched. The figure was hard to distinguish, for it perched upon the precipice to my left and shone in similar manner. At that distance, it was as if someone held a mirror up to the sun. However, somehow I felt sure that this image of light was another presence.

Just then, a whim made me think to look down at myself. Or was it more than that? It was as though a message had reached me from that strange being upon the far cliff. Suddenly I was overwhelmed by the thought that I should examine my own form, which before had been so shadowy and ethereal.

No longer. Now it was quite as solid as the ground beneath me. In colour, or absence of colour rather, it was like the twin pillars. My torso was reminiscent of a shell, armoured with great, interlocking plates. I raised my hand. It was a hand no longer. Like my body, it was encrusted, and my fingers were gone – fused into a great pincer.

Strange to tell, in my dream none of this dismayed me. I must have been monstrous, and the memory chills me now. But there was something in the tone of that ever-present voice from beyond the gate that lulled my doubts. More than that – it flattered me.

I can't say for certain what roused me then. Amidst so much awfulness, what detail stirred enough revulsion to jolt me into wakefulness? I wish I knew.

For sooner or later I'll have to sleep again. If I understood what might wake me from such half-known terrors, perhaps the prospect would appal me less.

Cha Né had spent the afternoon in preparation.

In shallow dreams he had hunted upon the shadow-lake for Shanoctoc, hoping against hope that his only agent in the Otherworld hadn't truly abandoned him. When Henry

Johnson had encroached upon the Endless Gate, the shaman and his spirit guide had consulted for two days, planning for every eventuality. Could the approaching threat really be so much worse? Could it intimidate even such a thing as Shanoctoc?

Cha Né woke with no answers to his questions. Angry and dispirited, he'd begun to make arrangements of his own. He had already gathered the ingredients he'd need. The base constituent was water from the lake, for it belonged almost as much to the Otherworld as to his own. The most powerful was the root of the Malaka, which grew in a single patch upon the far shore. But there were many other components, most virulent if used in the wrong proportions, and so the process of preparation was a slow one.

Finally, Cha Né removed his loincloth and his ceremonial garments, retaining only the charms he wore around his neck. Naked and squatting before the blazing hearth, he proceeded to rub the ointment into his body and face. Only when he was sure that he was entirely coated did he allow himself to relax, to meditate.

He felt the salve begin to dry, to work itself subtly within him. The pain rose slowly – until the heat beneath his flesh exceeded the blast of the fire without.

Cha Né held himself still. He remained calm. And eventually, the pain subsided. The heat inside him faded; so did the warmth from outside. All sensation died, by slow degrees. At first, it was like falling out of the world, like sinking into numbing water. But even those comparisons required feelings that, moment by moment, were lost to him.

Then unexpectedly, abruptly, it was over. The descent into deepest trance, the near-death of mind and body, was complete.

When Cha Né opened his eyes again, he was within the Otherworld.

Day 28

Eventful as they've been, only now do I find a moment to write of these last two days.

Yesterday we passed through the lands of the Lam. The tribe did nothing to hinder us, and we saw little sign of their presence. We camped without disturbance, and early this morning came upon the edge of the plateau.

I confess that I'd been expecting further bad dreams during the night, and their absence had left me in good cheer, perhaps even a little giddy. Yet as I looked out from those jungle-trimmed heights my excitement turned to ashes.

The view was unmistakably that of my nightmares from the night before. Across from us, where the cyclopean steps had descended, a river tumbled through the brush. The waters of the lake, whilst not so variedly coloured, were of equally vivid blues and greens. The cliffs were of similar proportions, though of unspectacular grey stone. As for the two black pillars, I saw two great rocks, one to either side of the distant river at the point where it met the lake.

Once the first flush of alarm had passed, I forced myself to consider how my imagination had so accurately anticipated geography I'd never seen. Surely, my subconscious mind must have pieced together details from Johnson's journal and the crude maps drawn by Middleton. It was hard to believe, but I could think of no other rational explanation.

Just as I'd managed to calm myself, the Lam descended upon us.

In my state of agitation, I almost fired on them with my revolver. I might really have done so if Harris hadn't caught my arm. As soon as he did, I realised what the others had seen already: we were not being threatened. No man in the delegation was less than ancient. These were the tribal elders, and they wanted only to talk.

Without our guides, however, even that was no easy task. I managed as well as I could with my smattering of the language. As far as I could tell, they were trying to warn me. I say that without egotism, for they spoke to no one else, though I'd done nothing to identify myself as expedition leader. They talked of a door, or so I thought, and they pointed often toward the twin rocks at the river outlet. But beyond that, I could make no sense of it.

When they realised their appeal was beyond my understanding, their manner grew more excitable. Finally, tired of their ranting, I insisted to the others that we continue onward, before the day was altogether wasted.

We left the elderly tribesmen shouting and pleading at our backs and began our descent. Whenever I glanced behind, I could see them watching from on high, and the sight unsettled me more than I could explain. I was glad when our progress cut them off from view.

The plateau proved lower on this side. By noon, we'd reached the heavily jungled rim of the basin. We could clearly see our objective, the lakeside village of the Shanopei, as a clutter of shelters upon the far shore. However, it was evident that there was no direct route between us and it. The only way down was to circumnavigate the basin and descend alongside the distant river, passing the mysterious twin obelisks. After the tirade I'd endured from the tribal elders, that prospect unsettled me more than it should have. But on another, perhaps more academic level, it intrigued me. I couldn't help wondering what secrets those barely-visible hieroglyphs might hold.

Intellectual curiosity, of course, won over. Against the protests of my companions, I insisted we make haste, so as to camp upon the lower level.

While we marched, I chided myself for being so easily unsettled by the recollections of a lunatic and the prattling of natives. They are wild people here, with wild ideas. My role as a rational man is to suck the poison from those concepts, so that more restrained minds can inspect them without threat of harm or infection. Re-reading my previous entries, I see to what extent I've failed in that regard – how I've allowed myself to fall under the sway of phantasms.

Well, no more. I am a man of science again. The travails of our day's journey have worn me out, but in that weariness I discover an unexpected depth of peace. As we make camp beneath a purple sky, and before those great carven rocks, I find myself calm for the first time in longer than I can remember.

In the fading light, those vast columns have a surprising, uncanny beauty. From my position by the campfire I can just discern the rows of pictograms that reach from base to tip. Perhaps they offer one more version of the fantasies that so dominate the lives of these people.

Whatever the case, they're a mystery for tomorrow. I feel serene, and very drowsy. Twice I've lain down to sleep. But there's a noise here, a curious, incessant murmuring. The others tell me I'm hearing the river. I'm certain, though, that it was more audible when we examined those twin rocks this afternoon.

The sound, however, is more soothing than distracting. I'll try to ignore it – or stop struggling with it, rather. Tomorrow will be the crucial day of our expedition. Tomorrow is what I came so very far for.

I must try to rest.

I must sleep.

Cha Né perched upon the Sun-drenched Cliffs.

He was deep within dream, so submerged that his body was only a fragile memory. He had torn through membranes of space and time, through many shades of consciousness. The way back was tortuous, hard to recollect.

The sky above was blank and cold. The luminous waters below curved and swelled against brilliant rocks.

Cha Né waited. Finally, in a distant flickering of

darkness, the avatar of the thing behind the Gate entered the Otherworld. It sparked into being upon the kaleidoscope of the lake and began immediately toward the Gate, regardless of the shifting surface beneath its hooves. It moved with an awkward creeping motion, bowed beneath its carapace, claw-arms clacking rhythmically. The Gate surged and writhed in anticipation.

Cha Né allowed the thing to approach. When it was close, he rose and moved cautiously nearer, casting vast shadows. The avatar didn't notice him at first; but when he leapt again, this time landing clenched in its path, it raised its snout and gave a scratching cry.

Cha Né squatted between the avatar and the infinite darkness of the Gate. It tried to manoeuvre around him, claws outstretched, head held low to protect its one cloudy eye from his brilliance. Cha Né shifted, keeping between it and the Gate. His thoughts, as he reached toward it, were a tangible thread of light that quivered in the ether.

Cha Né could feel the mind of the man, Montague Evans – like a dream or the memory of a dream. It no longer controlled the form encasing it. Cha Né felt the man's fear and recognized it as his own. He knew as well the price, should the thing behind the Endless Gate be unleashed. He had no choice. Burn out the mind of the man and the cancerous presence anchored to it would be vanquished too.

Cha Né faltered.

He could still taste the acid tang of what he'd done to Henry Johnson, of intelligence ground down to violent madness. What if this one were different? What if he could be reasoned with? Turned back? Could be saved?

Even as Cha Né thought this, the avatar scented his reluctance – the instance of weakness it had anticipated. In that moment, it lunged. The viscous web of its consciousness clutched at Cha Né, a cloud that howled around, within him. He felt his form fracture. He felt the drag of his body, the empty shell still squatting in the invented world.

He'd come too far, too deep. He couldn't remember the path back.

Broken, leaking light, Cha Né lay buoyed upon the liquid ground. The avatar didn't concern itself with him. It continued its creep to the Endless Gate, its milky eye still diverted, but its claws now clicking steadily again.

Cha Né's senses were failing. He saw the world as through a crust of ice. Yet he could still feel the umbilical cord of consciousness between himself and Montague Evans. He concentrated, focusing upon a last, hopeless transmission. He pressed through insect-thoughts, through drone-thoughts, into the screaming red of human mind below.

Even then, they had no language in common. They were so different. Could emotion bridge that gap? Could despair? "Free it in this world and you free it in our world. Montague Evans, listen to me... it will devour *everything*..."

Then the link was broken, melting into translucent dusts. If the avatar, or the mind of the man encased in it, had understood, it showed no sign. The thing continued its warped motion until it stood before the undulating black of the gate. The surface bent in dreadful curves as the avatar reached for the hieroglyphs of the pillar. The darkness throbbed, rolled out like storm clouds. Soon the creeping thing could no longer be seen amidst the pulsing ebon swell. But where it had been, something else was emerging – condensing.

Cha Né couldn't move. He couldn't look away. He could only lie still, watching.

It had been imprisoned for countless moons – for time beyond time.

It must be ravenous.

Day 29

My dreams last night were awful beyond imagination. I'm sure of this. Yet, I can't remember – or only the most indistinct details. A black and vacuous gateway. A strange, bright being, which spoke to me perhaps. Terror. Joy.

My memory is like a tattered cloth. Better to remember nothing than these half-grasped horrors, these flash-bulb grotesques that seem to be the shattered memories of a stranger.

Of the many things that petrify me this morning, this is the worst – this terrible sense of dislocation. I feel I've witnessed something dreadful. Maybe I even played a part. But that part is a void inside me. It belongs to someone – to something – else.

We've arrived at the village of the Shanopei. They would be unknown to the world were it not for Henry Johnson. Their evil superstitions would never have left this sheltered cove. Yet Johnson came, as I have come. Those superstitions have spread, as typhoid spreads.

This is what I sought. Now that I'm here, I can't but question my motives, and their repercussions. I told myself it was the correlations between my work and Johnson's that drew me. These are the reasons I offered my companions. Half-truths at best. It wasn't Johnson's theories that brought me but his madness. No, not even that. The cancer in his mind, the darkness that finally devoured his sanity... that was my lure. I opened my mind to the blackest dreams. Now I think those things may consume me.

The village of the Shanopei is gone. Only gutted remains survive, scorched in impossibly arbitrary fashion. There are no bodies, though the paraphernalia of life suggests the recent presence of people. There is nothing alive here. We can't even hear the singing of birds.

This was not the work of men. There are no tracks. It's

as if some force fell on the village, and desolated it, and was gone.

I fear it hasn't gone far.

The sky is crimson and purple and black, as though blood were bruising behind it. It's cold, so cold that the ground is hard, though yesterday we sweltered beneath tropical sun. The waters of the lake are viscous, swirling outward from the centre. They give the impression of appalling depths. Tendrils of fog rise from the water to gather about our feet. There's a carrion scent in the air, a murmuring that is something like music. The sky is without colour. The cliffs, through the mist, are crystalline.

I'm hallucinating. But the others claim they see the same. I can make out the bay; the canoes tethered there, the ravaged village, the river tumbling through mud flats into translucent water. Another scene lies on... over... *through* that one. At first, I could distinguish them. Now they seem to coexist.

The others want to retreat back toward the plateau. They insist I stop writing and go with them. I wish I could. I'm frozen, by awe and fear, and by the need to leave some record in the face of what I fear.

I remember Henry Johnson, tethered deep in the bowels of the asylum. The word he'd been calling incessantly since his arrival – and they told me his throat was cracked and torn by then, that it was a miracle he could make any noise at all – I believe that word was a name. *Astasoth.* I've known its meaning, I think, all along. I could have understood. I chose not to. *The imprisoned one.*

I'll leave this journal here. If I don't survive, perhaps it will. I hope it's never discovered. I hope it's lost forever. I can't tell any more what's real, what's delirium. The lake is obsidian, bubbling and frothing, flailing the shore with fluid tendrils. Beyond the beach, a well leads further down than I can see.

Something is rising.

I can't see. The fog devours everything. I hope it isn't real, that I'm insane. I'll follow my companions, to the path that leads up the cliff side. What else can I do? This wasn't my fault. A record – a record, at least. In the face of it. What else?

I hope this journal won't be found. I hope I'm mad. Let me die in the jungle, and rot, and never be remembered. Let me die mad and forgotten!

I fear I'm sane. I fear...

I know. Astasoth is free.

And it has other plans for me than death.

~

"The Door Beyond the Water" is at its core another early tale, one from a time when I was heavily in the thrall of Lovecraft, Poe, Machen and weird tales in general – a period that would provide the backbone and impetus for what would eventually end up being this collection. Like "The Facts in the Case of Algernon Whisper's Karma", it first appeared in a briefly-lived, little-read market called The Willows, *and like "The Facts in the Case of Algernon Whisper's Karma" it got something of an overhaul before I felt it was ready to stand alongside more recent work.*

In the case of "The Door Beyond the Water", however, that work had been done in advance and was a lot more comprehensive. I originally rewrote this one when I was approached by editor Eric Guignard to provide a story for his anthology Dark Tales of Lost Civilizations. *(Eric, incidentally, would publish another story from the collection, "Prisoner of Peace", in his next anthology,* After Death, *which would go on to win a well-deserved Stoker award.) Having nothing new to offer, Eric and I agreed that I'd revise an older piece under a new title, with the understanding that it would be a substantial enough revision to warrant the change of name.*

It turned out to be a welcome excuse to really set about tearing a story down and building it back up, and the results were satisfying. I was fond of the original, but the revision brought the things I liked about it into far sharper relief. As I've said, the impulse behind a lot of these stories was to write slantwise homages, pieces that stayed true to classical weird tales while finding new ways into their subject matter. In that sense, "The Door Beyond the Water" was me attempting to lock horns with the assumptions about race and civilization that are prevalent in so much genre fiction from the period. It's a tale of that classic Victorian educated white chap coming into a situation he doesn't even slightly understand and making one unholy mess of things, basically – and also, now that I think, an excuse for me to play around with some of the fascinating shamanism stuff that came out of studying Elizabethan witchcraft for my post-graduate degree.

Caretaker in the Garden of Dreams

Hunching his shoulders against the bitter wind, Gug-Shabeth gazed out over the long field. When he tutted beneath his breath, the Ka birds stirred in alarm from the branches overhead, circled once amidst the twilight sky, and then returned to their perches to glare down at his tumescent head with belligerent crimson eyes.

They didn't fear him. After all, why should they? They could easily dodge any attack his malformed arms might make.

Gug-Shabeth returned his watery stare to the long field. There, other birds had nestled amongst the crop, their leathery wings tucked around them like cloaks, their proboscises probing the strange fruits that grew there.

The scarecrow he'd built was nothing now but a cruciform frame draped with scraps of greying meat.

He was failing in his responsibility. But if they had ever intended him to succeed, ever cared at all, then they would not have made him so carelessly; every thought, every step, would not be such torment. No, the gods had little time for this patch of their creation, if indeed they had time for any of it, in their wantonness and their cruelty.

Still, what he lacked in form did not change his function.

Gug-Shabeth trudged painfully down the mound and onto the field, felt his feet drag down into the ebon soil. The nearest Ka took flight and circled warily, their tiny faces expressing outrage at the interruption of their meal. When he grunted at them, they dispersed resentfully to wait him out in the trees. With all the time in the world, they could afford a little patience.

Gug-Shabeth turned his attention to his crop. Each chi

was roughly spherical, its root invisible beneath the earth. Each was translucent, and visible within was layer inside layer, until at the very centre there shone a blue flame that shimmered and flowed. Some shone brightly, others only dimly. Every so often, one would flicker out altogether, and in an instant the shell that housed it would rot and congeal into the earth as if it had never been. Many others showed signs of where the Ka birds had fed. The outer leaves were split and raggedy or gouged away altogether.

From those nearby, Gug-Shabeth selected the chi that glowed most palely. He dug into the hard earth until the stump of its root was exposed, levered it free and tucked it under one arm. Above, the Ka birds whistled their protest. How dare this shambling thing touch their food? Annoyed as much by the pain in his gnarled fingers, Gug-Shabeth turned his face to the stars and howled in fury, and the birds spun skywards in a whirl of panic and charcoal feathers. He glared after them for a moment, and then trudged back across the field, the uprooted chi still cradled beneath his arm.

Laboriously, Gug-Shabeth clambered over the stile that crossed the fence and dropped heavily to the ground on the other side. The path was barely visible as a stain stretching into the darkness. Arriving at the foot of the hill, he crossed the bridge there, ignoring the cloying lap and sugary scent of the waters running beneath his feet. Beyond, the path rose again, but he bent his weight into the incline and gritted his mangled teeth and made no sound of complaint; for who was there to listen, or to care?

Finally he came to the peak of the rise, and beyond stood his home, and the garden that grew about it, nebulous as ever under the perpetual twilight.

Gug-Shabeth sat the chi on a rock and stared at it intently, until he was sure its flame still burnt, however slightly. Satisfied, he turned his attention to the meat-garden. Though it had been here when he'd first arrived, it was he who had nurtured the garden and had built his home beside it. While it was his, to use as he saw fit, he harvested its produce only when he had to.

Milky orbs gazed back at him from beneath frayed, pink leaves; bleached femur branches dwindled to thin tibia and patella; finger-bone twigs grew in weedy clusters; and everywhere hung bunches of moist red orbs, their thick sap dripping to clot in the tissue-grass.

Gug-Shabeth set about his task. He took windfall where he could, or picked from the lowest branches and from the ground foliage. Still, his muscles ached terribly, particularly his hopelessly crooked back.

Yet once he began to work there was nimbleness in his fingers, and he partly forgot the pain. The more he crafted, the more his discomforts subsided, the faster his knotted fingers spun in the damp air; for once Gug-Shabeth had been a fine craftsman, and though he didn't remember those times, yet some part of him awoke sometimes and worked marvels.

Soon, where he laboured in the clearing at the heart of the garden, there was another body before him. If its dimensions were strange, it was better made at least than he himself.

Gug-Shabeth stood back with a rumble of satisfaction.

He returned to the stump, checked the chi one last time and saw it was still lit, though barely. He carried it back to the clearing with both hands. When he reached the still body, he knelt over it and dug his nails deep into the skin of the chi, prising it in two with a sigh of exertion. Softly hissing, it split like an eggshell, and the glimmer of flame dripped out and into the open mouth of Gug-Shabeth's creation.

For a long while afterwards there was nothing but the sigh of wind in the bleeding willow, and the croak of distant insects. Then the thing opened its eyes and stared up at Gug-Shabeth and screamed.

It lay screaming for what seemed an age. But eventually the noise became hoarse, and was strangled off with a gurgling cough. Gug-Shabeth sat patiently on his haunches and waited. At last the thing sat up, glanced fearfully about, and said in a voice hardly above a whisper, "This isn't right. I'm not supposed to be here."

Gug-Shabeth, whose sharp teeth were crammed haphazardly into his mouth and whose tongue was a useless stump, could not speak to answer. Instead, he stood up and started towards the gate of the garden, and motioned for the thing to follow. After a while it fell in behind him.

"There was an accident," it said, "I remember an accident. And then... darkness, for a long, long time."

Gug-Shabeth grunted sympathetically, and started up the path beyond the gate. The thing he'd made followed nervously behind him, speaking in snatches, not seeming to care that he didn't answer it.

"Am I dreaming?" it asked. "Is this a nightmare?"

He led the way down the incline and over the bridge, up the hill beyond and between the trees and over the ancient stile, and all the while the thing mumbled to itself and asked questions that he had no means of answering. When they stepped onto the packed black earth of the long field, it said, "Am I dead? Am I in hell?"

Gug-Shabeth shook his head and pointed towards the crucifix at the centre of the field. The chi-thing gazed back at him with anxious eyes, then crossed over to the dilapidated frame and inspected it warily. Gug-Shabeth came up behind it, caught hold of one foot and lifted it into position upon the lower bar. He strapped the foot in place with the thong of leather hung there, and turned his attention to the other.

"What are you doing?" the thing asked nervously.

It made as if to struggle, then seemed to think better of it, and glared at him instead. As his creation, it couldn't resist him, any more than Gug-Shabeth could defy his own function. He eased its arms into place across the wide crossbar and bound those too.

The creature flailed a little, testing its bonds. Finding it could move no more than its head, it began to wail softly.

Gug-Shabeth wasn't without pity. But he understood necessity, and knew too that his little construction housed a chi that would soon have faded and passed. He had merely borrowed it a while from the order of things. Its suffering would be short and worthwhile.

As he walked away, back towards his home amidst the meat-garden, he could hear the thing screaming behind him, as the first of the Ka birds settled on it. A living chi fascinated them, so much so that they would abandon the easy, plentiful pickings growing around them. Yet it would take them a long while to search out their prize from its prison of flesh. He had hidden it carefully, and deep.

For that while, his crop would be safe.

Soon enough he would have to build another, another construct of meat with one fading chi nestled within it as sacrifice to keep its kin safe – soon, but not yet.

And for a time at least, Gug-Shabeth could rest his weary bones and be at peace.

~

The thought that first springs to mind in regards to "Caretaker in the Garden of Dreams" is that it came out of the same bout of insomnia – or maybe, rather, waiting-to-fall-asleep-weirdness – that produced my first novel Giant Thief, *and so its sequels, and so basically my entire career to date. Which is quite a lot of emotional weight to lay on one fairly short short story!*

Of the two, though, "Caretaker" is without a doubt the piece that feels like it was cobbled together out of random cerebral flotsam on the verge of sleep. Which is to say, it's downright odd; so odd that I find it odd and I wrote it! I know that I tried not to overanalyse things when I was writing it, making "Caretaker" one of those tales that I'd be pushed to offer any kind of definitive explanation of. My gut feeling is that the Long Field is an afterlife of sorts, but of course the title contradicts that. Perhaps, then, the chi represent those in comas, and poor Gug-Shabeth has the sad responsibility for deciding who'll one day wake and who never will. Whatever the case, I don't envy him his job.

A side note: isn't one of the cool things about horror is that it's where the monsters get to have a voice? I think maybe that's so. Certainly the pleasure of writing this one, other than how fundamentally strange it is, was that I got to describe some horrible things from a perspective so divorced from our own that you barely realise how nasty much of what happens is until you step back to think about it. Gug-Shabeth isn't a bad guy, but he certainly commits some impressively horrid acts before "Caretaker in the Garden of Dreams" is out.

A Twist Too Far

I know the police are seeking me. Small wonder!

Yet this is not a confession. Perhaps I'm a criminal, in an obscure sort of way, but what I did I did with as much reason as any man ever had. Nor did I flee from guilt, or to avoid justice. No, it was horror that drove me into seclusion – a horror that's never far from my mind. I sit beneath a Mediterranean sun, with the lap of warm waters close to my ear, and still that maddening sound hovers always on the edge of hearing...

I must try to tell things in order. Then perhaps you may understand, at least a little. I can live with the rest, if this half-existence can truly be called living. But I know I could never stand a prison cell, where I would have nothing to distract me. I can bear my guilt. I could not tolerate silence.

The beginning, at any rate, is easy to place. I met Fortesque through Mademoiselle de P_____, in the October of 19__. She was in her heyday then, performing the length and breadth of the Continent and into America too, wherever there was a flame of culture to guide her moth-like flight. We were old friends, sharing a past entirely unrelated to her celebrity. On that chill autumnal evening, we were taking quiet drinks in the back rooms of the Belladonna Club when he happened to chance by.

"Frederick!" she called. "You must join us!"

I recognised his thin frame and violently angled features from his advertisement posters, which just then were plastered all over London, and was immediately sceptical. Contortionism did not strike as a very intellectual or worthy art.

As though sensing my disapproval, Mademoiselle cried,

"Frederick, do please! You must meet my darling Victor. He shares not only your interest in orchid growing, but your passion for that dreadful Baroque music you insist in forcing upon me."

My ears pricked up. I've always been a solitary sort, having little in common with the mass of men. That anyone, let alone a seeker of publicity such as Fortesque, should be interested in not one but two of my passions – but it was quite true. We conversed late into the night, until poor Mademoiselle was no doubt fearfully bored; much brandy had been drunk, and a tentative companionship had taken form. I realised almost immediately, despite my cynicism, that he was a fellow of rare character.

We began to spend a deal of time together after that, first meeting in bars and gentleman's clubs and then visiting each other's apartments. We quickly found that we had more than those two pastimes in common, and abandoned talk of our great shared passions to explore these other, lesser fascinations. Then, over time, even our emphasis upon these similarities of character waned and we found we had become simply friends.

Fortesque took it upon himself to educate me on the intricacies of contortionism: of the subtleties of frontbending and backbending, of enterology and the professional's disgust at dislocations and other such cheap tricks. I soon discovered that contortion, like any trade perhaps, has unfathomable depths beneath a surface of simplicity. I learned too that even then, amongst his peers, Fortesque was an athlete of remarkable ability. It wasn't for nothing they called him the Human Knot. He could flow like water in a breeze; rearrange himself as though his limbs were some puzzle carelessly manipulated.

Yet he was not happy. I saw that the moment we met, and the certainty only grew upon me. His eyes were haunted. His moods were fiercely changeable. He would drink, sometimes, as though he fervently wished to be dead.

I would try to question him, of course. "Frederick, something bothers you."

"What? No, Victor, just this miasmal London weather."

"You seem perturbed."

"I'm nothing of the kind."

Fortesque, it struck me, was a man in great need of a confidant. Yet however much I probed or expressed my concern, he did not confide. I had lost a brother-in-law to monomania some years before, and knew enough to recognise the symptoms. He was in the grip of a commanding fervour, and I felt earnestly that without my aid it might consume him.

I was witness to this mania the first time I visited his apartments, though I couldn't recognise it then. We'd been sitting for an hour, sipping fine claret, when there came a knock upon the door. Fortesque flew to his feet, marched over, and flung it open.

There in the doorway, beside the butler, stood a most unexpected gentleman: an Indian in flowing robes and turban, a silky black beard hanging almost to his waist, an inscrutable expression on his weatherworn features. They conversed in whispers for a minute, Fortesque making no attempt to introduce me to his remarkable guest. Finally, he handed over a small, jingling bag. The man snatched it away, turned abruptly and was gone.

Fortesque gave a weary sigh, closed the door and resumed his chair. "You must excuse me."

"A matter of difficulty?"

"Oh, profoundly so. Still, let's not allow it to spoil our evening."

Though he made a show of jollity for the remainder of the night, I could tell that his mind lay elsewhere. Afterwards, the incident stayed in my thoughts, as a mystery to theorise upon whenever I wondered at my friend and his disturbances of character.

My first guess was that he was being in some way

extorted for money, and that suspicion was exasperated when a month or so later the Indian gentleman visited again. There followed a similar scene, and another exchange of what could only be coin, ending as before with the fellow's swift exit.

"If you are in any trouble, Frederick..."

"Trouble, Victor? None that I haven't imposed upon myself."

"If you're being pressured..."

"Pressured?"

"For money."

He laughed abruptly. "Ah, I see what you must think. No, the man is in my employ – and a very conscientious servant too. He's taking my part in negotiations for something, a certain substance, very much out of the ordinary... but I won't bore you with the details. It's a professional matter, and we're supposed to be at our leisure."

I nodded, tried to share his forced jollity. I didn't believe him in the least.

Yet, he was being perfectly honest. I should not have doubted my friend. I may never know the exact details, but I can piece much of it together with the benefit of hindsight.

All through that year there had been another contortionist performing in the capital, a self-proclaimed fakir going by the name of Cobra Bhatti. He was a remarkable talent, shrouded in mystery, and the papers had responded deliriously.

All of this, of course, was hardly beneficial to my friend's career. I thought it to his utmost credit that he expressed no jealousy or cynicism. He took me once to see the enigmatic fakir, and throughout the performance regaled me with thrilled observations on his adversary's every manoeuvre. For my own part, my heart sank further with each passing moment. I understood enough by then to see that Fortesque, for all his brilliance, was not this man's match. He was superior in terms of artistry and showmanship; yet Cobra Bhatti bent with seeming ease into forms no ordinary man should possess.

After one particularly remarkable stunt, I couldn't help but utter to myself, "Impossible!"

"Do you think so?"

"His spine... and the shoulder, even if it were entirely dislocated..."

"Well, I think you're partly right. Not physically possible, at any rate. Still – the man is a wonder."

My first reaction was to be impressed by the good nature with which my friend watched a competitor trounce his own extraordinary efforts. It was only later that the exact wording, the perplexing statement that Fortesque had made so casually, truly struck me.

If I respected Fortesque's lack of envy, I couldn't deny that his behaviour grew stranger after that night. I assumed that the caging of his rancour was what had soured his moods; that he was eaten inside by what he couldn't outwardly admit. It pains me to say that I understood my friend hardly at all. He was better than I ever gave him credit for – though perhaps less sane.

The year grew short, and our acquaintance vacillated. Cobra Bhatti's fame grew as Fortesque's waned, and there came upon me with each visit a sense of unease, a weight upon my heart.

He would be sometimes very jolly, sometimes barely communicative and almost stuporous. Twice more the Indian gentleman came to the door, and then Fortesque became animated in a way he never was by our discussions. Curiosity held me more than any pleasure in our time together. I developed new theories: he was in love with some lady of dubious virtue; he was absorbed in some criminal activity; or, more fitting to the facts, that he was an addict, pursuing some obscure opiate.

November fell like a shroud, bringing unseasonal cold,

flutters of snow and scathing winds. The days seemed briefer than they should be, more akin to the depths of winter. Fortesque's mood fell further. He would not perform. He did not go out. I expected every meeting to be our last. Yet every time he would end with a show of joviality, enthusiastically bidding me to come again, not resting until a date had been agreed.

Thus it was that I arrived that Thursday, with my coat white-flecked, my hat blown off-kilter. He shook my hand as though we were strangers. "So good to see you. You're brave to venture out."

"I've suffered nothing a brandy wouldn't cure."

He forced out a laugh and led me through to the study. It was a glorious room, all green leather and red wood, books piled everywhere; but just then, it had the air of a mausoleum. I took my usual chair and shuddered, pretending the outside chill to be the cause.

Fortesque looked macabre in his sharply cut black suit. He was nothing but skin wrapped over bones by then, and that skin was deathly pale. He poured us drinks. He seemed in a better mood than usually, though there was an air of mania to it, an awful energy.

"I didn't think you'd come. You have been very good, and more than that, persistent. I, for my part, have been taxing beyond reason. Well, no more of that."

"You exaggerate. You certainly do seem brighter, though."

"Brighter? Victor, have you ever wanted something so terribly that you thought it would kill you?"

"I can't say I have."

"No?" He seemed taken aback. "Well I have."

"Will you tell me what?"

"Oh, fame, glory... No, not that. To endure. To surpass what anyone has achieved. The farther I've progressed, the more I've come to resent this prison of meat I'm bound up in. My body has become a shackle and a terrible frustration.

I see the perfection of my art and am unable to achieve it. Can you understand?"

Choosing to think that he was talking, finally, of his unvoiced rivalry with Cobra Bhatti, I replied, "I think, a little."

"I would give everything. Money, property, affection – aren't those silly things, in the end? No, I see it in your eyes – not to you. Not to most men. If only they could be enough!"

"Perhaps, with rest and care, they would be?"

"I only wish..."

There came a knock upon the door: a funereal knell that made me start. Fortesque leaped to his feet as though electrocuted. He rushed across the room, flung open the portal, and nearly shoved his poor butler to the ground in his eagerness to reach the man behind him: the Indian gentleman, of course, as I'd known it must be.

"You have it!" Fortesque cried. "Oh, you have it. Won't you come in and join us? Share a drink?" I saw something change hands, but failed to make out the Indian's low-voiced reply. "No, no, I'm sorry... only you've done me such a service. What's that? You worry too much, sir. Well, it's understandable. I'll bid you goodnight, then."

The Indian turned away. I would never see him again. Fortesque slammed the door, went to resume his seat, jerked nervously back to his feet, flew to the dresser and placed there the thing he'd been holding. It was nothing but a small bottle of blue glass. So he really was an addict, after all. I was struck by a dreadful sense of disappointment at seeing my friend so reduced.

His eyes – staring now, almost fevered – swung in my direction, and he read the thought from my expression. "Victor, you have me wrong. It's nothing so base! Or perhaps it is – but not that, at any rate. The substance you see here is ancient, antediluvian even, and a thousand times rarer than any conventional drug. It lacks even a name. I had heard rumours, though, found mention of it in ancient texts. Only when I saw Cobra Bhatti for the first time did I truly believe in its existence. You realised yourself, even said as much, that no man could do the things he does unaided. I've been approaching him ever since through my colleague there, offering huge sums for the tiniest sample. He took my money, and gave nothing in return; an artist behaving like a cheap swindler! I arranged, finally, to take the matter into my own hands. Now there it is. A crook such as Bhatti doesn't deserve this. He could never truly exploit its possibilities."

I had no idea what to make of this speech, and whether I should believe it. In the end, all I could think to say was, "It sounds fearfully dangerous."

"Not so. Not if taken carefully."

"There are tests that might be made..."

"Enough, Victor! Can you really imagine I'd wait further, after all this time, to prove what I already know? I'm sorry. Forgive me. Only, you must understand what I've endured these past months. Of course – I shall try to be careful. Only, to abstain any longer..."

I took this as a hint. "I should leave you alone."

"I didn't mean that. You've only just arrived. Still... I doubt my company will be very engaging."

"We'll meet again soon, and you can show me the wonders you've achieved."

He walked over as I stood, and shook my hand once more. This time there was an earnestness to the gesture that I found touching. "We will, and I shall."

He ushered me to the door, trying and failing to disguise his urgency. The butler was elsewhere, and so he let me out himself, with a smile of forced jollity. The door shut behind me almost before I'd reached the safety of the step.

The snow still fell, heavier now, although the wind had died. Fortesque's narrow oblong of garden bore a dusting of white and the sky above was black as pitch, stars and flakes mingling in a glittering curtain. I took a few steps towards the gate, stopped – shivered. I couldn't escape a sense of dread. I remembered Cobra Bhatti, his awful contortions. How much more could a body endure? And what if the mind itself was already bent into convolutions?

I took two more steps, almost enough to reach the gate. I looked back. I told myself I was being foolish. I'd almost convinced myself – when I heard the sound.

How can I describe it? Its like has never been heard. There was the grind of a sausage maker in there, the wet slap of meat on meat, a clicking akin to a hundred dice thrown all together. My heart throbbed into my throat. I thought I'd vomit. Instead, I turned back, and ran.

I reached the door at full tilt and set to hammering with my fists. The butler seemed to take an age. He was flushed when the door eventually swung inward, near to panic himself. I didn't care. I pushed him roughly aside. I threw all my weight against the study door, expecting to find it locked, and stumbled when it flew open.

A whimper met my entrance, like water gargling up through a crack in rock. It came from the *thing*. It was on the floor, rocking as though in a breeze, twitching – a tangled ball of flesh.

There on the chair were his clothes, neatly piled. This was not Fortesque, though it had his face. It was not a man. The bottle lay on the floor, dribbling its last contents into the carpet.

The *thing* turned imploring, fluid eyes on me. The sagging mouth quivered. It raised a hand, on a wrist soft as jelly, tried to gesticulate.

This was not, could not be my friend.

Yet I knew that the word it was trying to form with those smashed lips was my name.

"No!"

There was an oil lamp burning above the mantelpiece. I dashed it to the floor. It spun against a bookcase, shattered, spewed its contents. A circle of the room lit up immediately. The books ignited, then the wood, and only seconds had passed before bright flames were licking the ceiling.

I looked once at the monstrosity that had been Fortesque. He was trying to say something. To thank me? I hoped so. Then the flames reached him. I turned away. His mangled screams broke like a wave against my back.

The rest is of little importance. I dragged the butler out, against his will. It is with him that this charge originates, no doubt. You must see that it can't be called murder. If anything, it was suicide, or, I fervently hope, a sad and foolish accident. I am sorry for it, fearfully sorry – and not for Fortesque only. You'll continue to pursue me, I don't doubt, you for whom justice can only be drawn in black or white.

Well, you will not find me.

I offer this condolence: My mind has constructed its own punishment.

That noise – of flesh and bone distorting into shapes they should never possess – I hear it behind the lap of the waves, the sough of breeze through the olive trees. I hear it in my dreams. I hear it always, and everywhere. I hear it now as I write.

It is the worst sound imaginable, and I will never escape it in this life.

~

Of "A Twist Too Far", I feel that all I should really have to say is, how creepy are contortionists? I mean, not as people, I'm sure they're lovely people, or at least only creepy in the normal ratios of creepiness to non-creepiness. But as a medium of entertainment, contortionists are pretty creepy. And it's plain amazing that there aren't more horror stories written about them.

"A Twist Too Far" sprang out of some similar impulses to "The Facts in the Case of Algernon Whisper's Karma", in that once again the narrator is a Watson to the protagonist's Holmes, looking on in awe, bafflement and eventually in horror as their idol goes further and further beyond the pale. In "A Twist Too Far", however, the object of the narrator's fascination is a

genuinely extraordinary individual – one who only gets more extraordinary as the story progresses – and the narrator is basically reliable, so far as these things go.

Beyond that, I think the impulse here, as a big fan of film director David Cronenberg, was to have a go at Edwardian body horror. As somebody who often doesn't remember their own work very well, I'm always a little surprised when I return to "A Twist Too Far" and discover just how nasty it gets by the end. In fact, as much as this one has the fingerprints of the usual suspects all over it – there's a bit of Wells in the style, a bit of Poe and maybe James in the content – I suspect that Cronenberg was my biggest influence. Certainly the story's questioning of how far you can distort the human body before it becomes something altogether other is one I'd like to think he'd approve of.

The Untold Ghost

My first impression of the Levinsham Park hotel was that it looked like something out of a horror film. It was architecturally eccentric, each extension added with no thought for the overall appearance, and that night there was just enough moonlight to make the place seem crooked, malformed, a little deranged.

Pulling up on the crescent of gravel driveway, I could see that the house had also been quite elegant in its day. There was a time when I'd have been impressed, but for the last couple of months we'd been exceptionally busy, and my firm had been overlooking all except the most preposterous bills to get me where they wanted at a moment's notice. Anyway, I was only there for the night. I had time for the briefest of acquaintances: a meal, and enough drinks to get me to sleep in an unfamiliar bed.

The foyer was panelled in dark wood, illuminated by lamps in green-paned casements, decorated with landscapes of desolate places under storm cloud skies. They were evidently striving for austerity; yet sat upon the stiff Edwardian chairs and dressers were an army of stuffed toy bears, varying from the tiny to the gigantic. They were old enough to suit their surroundings, pitiful threadbare creatures, but despite their age and weathering, they smiled sewn-on smiles and their black eyes glittered cheerfully.

Even that eccentricity didn't make the place seem very welcoming. Neither did the receptionist, with his comb-over and affected lisp. He was determined to have me fill in the visitor book, I was equally determined to be shown the bar, and we wrangled for a while before he eventually gave in. He was back two minutes later, with my glass perched on a tray in one hand, and slyly, the visitors book in the other. I filled it in while I sipped my whisky. The bar was an improvement over the entrance hall: spacious and comfortably furnished, with an open fire crackling in a lounge beyond a full-size snooker table. I gulped down the last of my drink and felt better.

My case was waiting where I'd left it, along with an elderly porter. He clutched my luggage and led me up the great flight of stairs to a landing. There, faded Chinese watercolours replaced the gloomy gothic paintings below. They were an insipid collection, probably European fakes. One picture did catch my attention, though: a pencil sketch of two young girls, which I think I noticed simply because the image seemed so out of place.

I only had time to glance before my guide's frown forced me on. We passed through another hall, climbed another set of stairs, and filed along two narrow corridors that twisted without apparent rhyme or reason. He ushered me finally into my room, leaving me to gaze gratefully at the colossal bed. Exhausted from the drive down, I could have happily fallen asleep. Instead, I forced myself into the bathroom and splashed water on my face until I felt I could stay awake for dinner.

Dinner, unfortunately, didn't seat until half past six. I made a tour of the room to pass some time, inspecting the miniature prints decorating the walls and the view over the gardens. The usual brochure was perched on the fireplace, with its mix of local tourist information, instructions for emergencies and exorbitantly priced services. I learned the foundations of Levinsham Hall dated from the late sixteenth century, when Isaiah Levinsham had constructed what formed the core of the current building. A proud family home for many generations, the house had only recently fallen on hard enough times to disgrace itself with the paying public.

Turning to the end, I wasn't surprised to discover that the Levinsham had its own ghost tale. It was a strangely bloodless one, though, even compared with the usual trite stories of translucent women wandering through the corridors. It began with the grandson of the original founder, his wife, and their staff returning from travels abroad. When the lady first went upstairs there was heard a scream, which all concerned reported to be blood curdling. By the time her husband found her, she was lying curled on the floor of the main bedroom. Despite his initial fears, however, he found that she'd merely fainted, and she was eventually brought round with smelling salts.

The author had made a half-hearted attempt to inject an air of mystery – 'the lady was never quite the same after that day' and such – but it was still uninspired and explainable in a dozen perfectly mundane ways.

I glanced at the clock and noted that it was barely past six. I considered another drink, and decided that a walk would do me more good. The grounds were impressive; I could easily waste half an hour exploring. I set off back towards the second-floor landing, following the first of the capriciously winding corridors. Taking my time, I noticed details I'd missed before. First was a door at the end of the passage, which drew my interest because it had been clumsily boarded up. That was understandable, perhaps a section of the house had become dangerous through disrepair, but still, the shoddy workmanship seemed out of place.

I made my next discovery around the corner: a short passageway off to the left, leading to a fire door, where a cardboard sign strung across the entrance read 'NO EXIT' in large black print. This was much stranger. I felt sure the door was in an outside wall, so where could it lead, and wasn't it irresponsible to cordon off a fire exit?

I suppose that indignation was how I justified what I did next, although I suspect it had more to do with bored curiosity. I climbed over the sign and gave the door a firm shove. It swung open. In the dim moonlight, I could see a narrow cast-iron balcony. It looked sturdy enough, so I stepped out, clutching the doorframe in case it should collapse.

The balcony ran to my left, where it met a tower set into the corner of the house – presumably, where the mysteriously barricaded door led. It seemed to be in good enough repair from the outside. A rickety spiral staircase led down to the ground at the point where the balcony met the tower. Ivy encrusted both tower and fire escape; perhaps why I'd failed to see them when I arrived, and why the stairs were deemed unsafe.

I turned back, my curiosity sated. Then some other urge – morbid fascination I suppose – made me want to glance over the edge. I crossed to the railing and gazed downward. I wasn't so high up, only two storeys, but the darkness and acute angle elongated the distance. For a moment my head spun. I tried to calm myself, thinking, *it's not so far. You wouldn't even hurt yourself, if you were lucky.*

A child though – for a child it would be a long way.

They could never survive.

I remember those precise words, though the thought seemed to come and go of its own accord. Suddenly I was very dizzy, much worse than before. I clutched the rail. I remember a feeling of awful pressure on my back. Struggling, I pushed away, and stumbled back through the open door.

Abruptly, my mind began to work again. I was very cold, my hands completely numb. It was late autumn, and I wasn't wearing a coat or gloves, but then I hadn't been out for more than a few seconds. I slammed the door, clambered clumsily over the makeshift sign, and collapsed against the wall, panting for breath, terrified one of the hotel staff would appear to interrogate me.

I calmed down fairly quickly and was as quick to blame the whole thing on an attack of vertigo. All I wanted was to get out of that corridor, to go somewhere warm and forget my stupid curiosity and its almost-disastrous consequences.

I resumed my journey as soon as I was sure my knees had stopped shaking. I noticed the picture again going downstairs, the sketch of the two girls. Again, something about it drew my attention, and this time I could see what it was. The piece was nothing special on the surface, a mix of pencil and charcoal by someone who favoured dark, harsh lines too much. The artist was no professional. More likely, it was the work of a parent trying to capture an image of their daughters for posterity. The girls were practically identical, even down to the trim of their hair and the cut of their collars. Their faces, caught between boredom and hesitant smiles, were much the same. They might have been reflections of each other. Except...

I admit that I still felt shaken, and tired from the day's driving. Yet it seemed to me there was a difference, a distinction too subtle for the heavy-handed artist to have caught deliberately. It had something to do with light and shade, with the curve of lips and the barest hint of expression in eyes. Its effect was simply that the girl on the right looked *wrong*.

I can't put it any better. You could replace the word wrong with bad perhaps, but I think that would be straying from what I thought in that instant. The effect was more as if the artist had tried to express a flaw they secretly suspected, or failed to hide something they sensed but couldn't admit.

It doesn't sound such a big deal. It sounds, I'm sure, like something I'd have imagined. Perhaps I did. Maybe it was only after what happened later that the sense of wrongness really struck me.

I marched on towards the dining room, thoughts of a walk long gone, hoping the kitchen would make some dispensation in view of my urgent appetite. I was surprised to see that the room had already begun to fill. A waiter brushed past as I stood in the doorway, and I asked whether the kitchens had opened early.

"Early? No sir."

"But it's –"

He waved towards a teak grandfather clock. "Twenty to seven sir. Can I show you to a table?"

I could only nod, and follow behind, tumbling into the chair he offered me. How had it taken me over half an hour to walk from my room? Had my dizzy spell lasted longer that it had seemed to? I ordered a bottle of merlot, downed the first glass almost in one gulp. I felt better after that, and capable of examining the menu. It was a set price, and I was glad I wouldn't be footing the bill. I collared the waiter again, and ordered the soup, with grilled salmon to follow.

The food, when it came, seemed magnificent. At the pace I wolfed everything down, though, it would have been a miracle if I even tasted it. I decided against dessert and heaved myself to my feet, leaving a decent tip safe in the knowledge that I'd charge it to my firm. I think I glanced at the picture once more as I went by. I know I shuddered when I passed the fire door, and hurried on.

Back in my room, I stripped to my underpants and stood wavering in the middle of the room, torn between the bother of having a shower then and the horror of getting up even earlier the next morning. I couldn't face the latter, so I stumbled into the bathroom.

I'd left it too late. Other, more punctual guests had exhausted the hotel's boilers. Accompanied by the clanking of strained plumbing, the water went rapidly from scalding to lukewarm to cold. I was shivering by the time I stepped out, and considerably more sober. I towelled myself roughly and slipped beneath the quilt, still rubbing furiously at my damp hair. Neither the heavy quilt nor my own efforts did much to warm me. I scrabbled into the depths of the bed, crushed my head into the pillow, and realised that sleep seemed very far away.

I opened my eyes and stared at the ceiling. I could

follow spider webs of hairline cracks in the plaster, and the geography of worm holes in dark wood beams. It was still freezing, even with the quilt tucked tight, and seemed to be getting colder. I lay shivering, hunting for patterns in the cosmos of stains and fractures above. It was almost like self-hypnosis. For moments, the exercise seemed to work, with my thoughts starting to muddle, my eyes drifting shut. But each time the cold would drill further into me and I'd snap back to wakefulness.

I don't know how long this went on for. I lay still, growing colder and colder, staring at nothing. Eventually, furious with frustration, I rolled onto my side.

A figure stood beside the bed. She was about four feet tall, a black silhouette against the bright gap of the curtains. I wasn't afraid, but the cold was horrible. I knew it was a little girl even before she spoke, knew without question. I think I also knew it was the girl in the picture.

She took a step closer, and I felt a small hand pressed into mine. It might have been carved out of ice.

"Will I be all right?" she asked. Her voice was distant and fragile, the last ripple of an echo.

"Of course," I whispered. But I knew I was lying.

She let go then, hesitantly, and I could feel her smiling even though I couldn't see it: A sad smile, full of tragic knowledge. She understood that I was lying too, and she didn't blame me. Still, the feeling of guilt was overwhelming. I had to turn away.

When I looked back, she was gone.

I've never returned to The Levinsham Park. On the one occasion I've stayed in the area since, I opted for the Poplars Guest House instead. It isn't extravagant or elegant, it has no ghost story in its cheaply photocopied brochure, but the landlady makes good lasagne, and their house red is quite decent.

I haven't been back to The Levinsham. I wouldn't. I

don't know what occurred that night, if anything did, if it wasn't a dream fuelled by wine and fatigue. I'd swear it wasn't – that I've never been more awake. But if it really happened...

I should say that I don't believe in ghosts – or at least I didn't. I can't deny what I saw, felt, and heard, or that for brief moments there were thoughts in my head that weren't my own. If any of that's true... well perhaps I've been wrong about a lot of things. That night has stayed in my mind despite my best efforts to forget. I hope writing it out will be a cure to that. Whatever happened, I'm tired of carrying the memory.

I believe that there's a mystery in the rooms and passages of The Levinsham Park. I believe that somewhere in its long history a child fell, and her father – lost to his own demons – failed to save her, or failed to try, or maybe even did worse than that. Either way, that tragedy left something that a subsequent generation has tried to hide, and maybe even to propitiate; with an absurd ghost story, barred doors, with an army of decaying toy bears. I've often wondered how many other near-accidents there were before the balcony was sealed off, wondered too about what lay in that shut-away tower.

There's a mystery at the Levinsham Park, but I've no interest in solving it myself. I've borne witness. I think that's all she can ask of me.

Perhaps something terrible happened, something clumsily hidden yet never forgotten.

Maybe there's a little girl there, or the faintest shadow of what was once a little girl.

And perhaps, in the depths of the night, she chooses not to be forgotten.

~

"The Untold Ghost" is surely the closest this collection comes to an actually autobiographical tale. The Levinsham Park was based on a real hotel that, frustratingly, I can't remember the name of, but which I ended up imitating

fairly closely. My first visit there was also the first time I'd stayed in anything approaching a posh hotel (paid for by my then-employer, thanks to a convenient training course) and it was quite the formative experience. If nothing else, it made me wish I got to stay in posh hotels more often!

However when I went back a few months later, the place seemed a lot seedier. I can't remember whether I wrote "The Untold Ghost" after my first or second visit, but if it was the first then I certainly picked up subconsciously on that sense of faded grandeur; reading back now, it feels entirely integral to the story. At any rate, a great deal of that hotel went into the Levinsham: the creepy teddy bears in the foyer were a borrowing, as was the bar, the generally labyrinthine layout and the description of the protagonist's room. I can't remember if the hotel had its own ghost story or if that detail came from elsewhere, but if it did then I suspect it was every bit as rubbish as the Levinsham's!

Embarrassingly, the protagonist's irresponsible behaviour is also based on my own. I was so intrigued by the place – not to mention, bored – that I decided to go exploring, even if it meant ignoring the odd 'do not open' sign. I eventually decided to pack in my exploring when I ended up on the roof, which perhaps makes me slightly more sensible than the narrator – or perhaps not. Sad to say, though, and as much as it would have been the perfect conclusion, the ghost was entirely made up, and I had no remotely spooky experiences whatsoever. It was a shame, because if ever a hotel was meant for such things it was that one. In fact, looking back, perhaps my main reason for writing "The Untold Ghost" was to address such an obvious oversight!

A Study in Red and White

Poised on snow-slicked roof tiles, the Santa Thing scents the wind.

The air reeks of snow. It licks across raw, red muscle and sinew, testing cavities and meaty crevices. The cold reminds the Santa Thing of home – and for a moment, it recalls older winters, deeper frosts, the uncluttered, frozen eons before shape and form and roiling, sickly life. An age when it seemed nothing would ever claw its way from the utter chill to crawl and mewl. An age when there was no need for subterfuge.

No time, no time for memory. Not tonight, most special and rich.

Here there's a simple way down – a jut of hollow masonry beckoning. Once, they burned fires in those depths. That recollection brings no comfort. But this is a different age and the blackness welcomes. Too narrow, though, for this current shape. No space for the Santa Thing's ebon hooves, no room for the curlicues of bone that splinter its face and cluster round its head. Change is needed, as it has changed so many times before.

It's a matter of a thought – for the Santa Thing is thought as much as matter, idea more than either. Flesh softens to jelly, to dripping wax. Muscle expands, contracts. A hundred bones click free. As they relocate, their note is faintly like the ring of bells.

Quick as light, quick as sorrow, the Santa Thing spills into darkness. It flows through gloom, where ancient ash still clings – slops into multicoloured light. A tree, strung and adorned. One of their Signs. Once the decorations were mistletoe sprigs, once the lights were candles and a ward. But humans don't remember as the Santa Thing remembers.

Now those flames are pretty and pointless. Though they sting the running jelly of its eyes, they can't keep the Santa Thing from entering.

Shuddering like an oil-slicked bird, the Santa Thing takes back its form. Already its helpers chitter from the shadows at its presence. Their half-life goes hard on them. They exist only for this moment. Now that it's come once more, they scud and shudder round the walls – flicker across cheap furniture, hung stockings, clumsily wrapped parcels.

The Santa Thing lets the moment drag, lets them drive themselves to the brink of frenzy with anticipation. Only when they seem about to tear themselves apart does it speak, its voice rich and foul with the pressure of ages.

"Gud ur Bad?" asks the Santa Thing. "Gud ur Bad?"

In unison, they shriek their answer.

The Santa Thing shakes its flayed head in mock censure. How they struggle, these humans – these bags of unshifting meat and forgetting. How they neglect the old rules, the forms laid down millennia before they skulked into the world.

Bad? Bad it is.

Its helpers quieten now, stilled by awe and all they understand of fear. So much waiting, just for this moment. Their dust-mote eyes stare from every patch and stripe of murk. The Santa Thing gathers itself, reaches deep into the roiling galaxies within its form. Time stands on edge. Bladders swell, organs secrete, and arteries aslant from space drip piceous fluids.

Upon the brink of two realities, the Santa Thing releases.

To its own eyes, impulse and sensation spew and spray across the walls: A word of anger here, a casual blow there, an urge to hate drying in a filthy birthmark. To its eyes, a map in space and time charts pain across the patterned wallpaper. The colours are rich, delightful. Yet, for those who'll live out this portrait, nothing they'll ever see. If only they could register its beauty, perhaps they could resist its lure.

A sound. A stutter of shock. The Santa Thing has let itself be distracted. Something has sneaked up, noiseless until the very last moment. Even as it spins, the Santa Thing twists, reforms, tries to become what they have made of it.

Still, the small creature framed in the empty doorway looks afraid. It shouldn't be here, it knows. Fear strikes it dumb. Its lips tremble ... a name hangs there. Not the Santa Thing's, but familiar. The name is a prayer. The prayer remains unspoken.

The Santa Thing hears nonetheless.

Forgive me, Father Christmas.

But the Santa Thing is father to nothing. Knowing what awaits this small creature, knowing what the new year will bring, it smiles its mouth round moist, shivering words.

"HaPee KrisMus. HaPree KrisMus, Litul One."

The Santa Thing doesn't wait for a response. Even for a being that lives between the cracks of time, there's much to be done this sacred night. It melts instead back into the darkness, a memory already fading and mixing with illusion in an infant mind that will never be quite sane again. Embracing the chill night wind, the Santa Thing flees for a star-slick sky, smears its long silhouette across a bulbous moon.

And in its wake, fluid with echo, trails a sound that might be laughter.

~

Oftentimes the impetus for a short story comes from either a dream — an awful writer cliché, but every so often dreams do chuck up the best ideas — or, more reliably, from the period when I'm just drifting to sleep and manage to wake up enough to scribble a brief, cryptic note to myself. So it was with "A Study in Red and White", and the note in question read simply 'the Santa Thing'.

The great thing about notes like that is that — when I can make sense of them by the cold light of day, which isn't always — they seem to act as a kind of shorthand to the subconscious. Those three words just clicked for me, and what came straight to mind was what would end up becoming "*A Study in Red and White*". Which is to say, when I read 'the Santa Thing' what I envisaged was Father Christmas reimagined as an immortal, pain-spewing horror-god from Earth's primordial past.

If nothing else, this probably explains why I'm a writer and not, say, a primary school teacher.

That said, I would argue that my version of Santa Claus is the only one that successfully reconciles all of the unlikely and contradictory details regarding everyone's favourite super-powered, Coca Cola-inspired, ever-jovial festive saint. So who knows? Maybe I was onto something with this one.

A Stare from the Darkness

It wasn't night.

Until night fell, at least, he was safe.

Werner hugged the pack to himself, more for comfort than to shelter it, since the contents were already sodden. The sky was a leaden grey, the rain harder than ever, and he missed his parents, ached with the knowledge that even if he returned they wouldn't be there waiting. There was nothing consoling in the bag: only the silver cross that had been his mother's, a wreath of garlic flowers, and a stake carved from live wood. He didn't believe they'd protect him. Now that the task was almost on him, he felt like a child lost in the woods.

Trudging through the gloom, looking down to keep the rain from his face and caught in remembered horrors, Werner finally came upon the castle without noticing. He paused to draw wet hair from his eyes and there it was, rising before him, a silhouette carved from the lighter darkness of the sky.

He had come out on the edge of the forest. A small courtyard lay ahead, and beyond that the edifice of the coast-fort. It was smaller than he'd imagined, built all of stone over two storeys, scarred badly by disrepair and weathering. A single arched doorway stood directly ahead, with what must be stables off to one side. There were no signs of life, no lights in the windows or smoke rising from the great outlying chimney.

Any attempt to think beyond this point had exhausted his imagination. Werner knew he couldn't simply walk in the main door. He felt sure it was still day, with an hour or more before nightfall, though it was even darker than before. If the stories were true, he had nothing to fear from the monster itself.

But it might have servants. They would see him approaching, if they hadn't already.

Werner ran to take refuge in the shadow of the wall, and crouched for a few moments, close to panic. When no shout came, he began to follow the stonework around. Just beyond the corner was a smaller door. He crept to it and listened. There was nothing to hear, however, beside the thrash of rain on stone. Werner scurried to one side and pushed the door a fraction ajar, just enough that he could glimpse inside. He could see nothing either, only blackness. The idea of entering that gloom was terrifying – but no more so than the thought of staying outside until night fell. He pushed the door further and slipped inside, still crouched on hands and knees.

He realised as his eyes adjusted that he was in a large kitchen, with wood-inlaid work surfaces round the walls, a grand table in the centre, and a great stove of black metal squatting in the far corner. He couldn't tell if anyone had used it recently. Though the creature would have no need for any food that could be prepared here, perhaps its retainers did.

There was no use in investigating, so he glanced about for a way onward. There was a low archway beside the stove and a second door ahead. The door would lead in the direction of the main entrance, so he crept towards the archway instead. There, stone steps led upwards. In the stories, the creatures slept in crypts or cellars, subterranean places where no one would discover them. Werner had no idea if there even was a lower level to the fort. In reality, it might rest anywhere, assuming the villagers would be too afraid to come here. The thought angered him, and his anger restored a little courage. He began to climb the stairs.

They opened onto a corridor that stretched left and right. In one direction, the passage turned a corner where it met the outside wall. In the other, it led out to a large landing, where the main staircase must be. Two doors stood before the opening, one to either side. Feeling exposed and close to panic again, Werner edged along the wall behind him, opened the door there, and slid inside.

The room beyond, though edged in shadow, was better lit than the corridor. The windows were thickly curtained, but a single candle stood ensconced on a chest beside the door. This unprecedented sign of life alarmed him, and his first thought was to hide. Glancing frantically around, he realised the room was almost empty besides the trunk – and its only other content paralyzed him where he stood.

A huge bed draped in red linens stood opposite. A body lay on the bed. Werner, afraid and confused, took in further details slowly: the figure was dressed in a robe stretching from its shoulders to drape around its feet; its forearms rested on its chest, hands folded together; and it was old, impossibly old.

That was all he could see from where he stood. Yet it was a long time before he could bring himself to move, and then the motion he made was almost imperceptible. The body didn't stir. Werner was sure now that it wouldn't – not until the sun fell beneath the horizon. He took another step, another, until he stood close to the bed's foot.

He only remembered then the bag slung over his shoulder. He clawed it open, suddenly frantic, dragged at the cross and wreath with numb fingers. The sodden wreath fell apart, and he dropped the bag. Werner fell to his knees and scrabbled until he caught hold of the crucifix. He dragged it around his neck. Then he lurched to his feet, with the stake in his right hand, clutched tightly enough to drive splinters through his skin.

The figure on the bed hadn't moved. Nor did it now, as he stared down at it.

Werner – seeing it so perfectly still, and the pallor of its face and wasted limbs – wondered for a moment at his fear. Yet soon, he knew, the creature would rise. Those frail arms would have strength. Those still, sunken eyes would open and would see him. The thought drove him to stumble forward, his weapon poised. But once beside the bed he could only stare, and try in vain to control the shaking of his hand.

He knew he should aim for the heart. He could see where the gown lay open – could even make out the ridges of the creature's ribs, the skin hanging sunken between them. He could see the precise spot he should strike. But he couldn't keep his hand from trembling. It would wake at any moment. It would kill him, as it had his parents. He would have failed. It would slowly drain the last life from his village.

Werner's fingers shook so much that he could barely hold the stake. He couldn't do it, couldn't take the life of something even so monstrous as this. He was lost, his village was doomed, and...

A noise came from the corridor, a scuff of movement, and in a fury of blind terror, he drove his arm downwards. The motion was so swift that it didn't seem his, yet at the same time, his arm appeared to drift ever so slowly through space – so that when the stake struck the old man's chest he felt every subtlety of the collision. He sensed flesh tear as the point drove into it, a tremor as the spike caught against a rib, a shudder as the bones pried apart. Then the tip sank into the heart, with a noise and sensation more awful than anything he could have imagined. Warm dampness welled between his fingers, and Werner knew it was blood, but he couldn't let go. He began to cry, in silent sobs. All he could see was his fist, the stake, the old man's ruined chest.

He heard the door open behind him, and a scream – which he realised eventually wasn't his, and stopped as abruptly as it had started. Only then did he manage to free his hand, to turn slowly around. A woman stood in the doorway, supporting herself with one outstretched arm against the frame. She was old, with grey hair hanging past her shoulders, and dressed entirely in black. Werner wanted to beg and plead to her, to tell her he was sorry, to hide his bloodied palms. He found that he couldn't make any noise at all.

She spoke instead. "I knew you'd come eventually. But you're too late."

For a while after that, Werner was only half-aware. A fog lay on the edge of his vision, and a ringing in his ears deadened any other sound. It didn't seem strange, as it would later, that the woman led him out of the bedchamber, through the corridor, down the stairs into the kitchen. It didn't surprise him when she warmed water and handed him a cloth to wash his hands. He accepted her explanation, "We can't talk with my husband's blood on you." He scrubbed and scrubbed, and wouldn't have stopped except that after a while she drew him away and ushered him into a chair.

Then he didn't remember anything for a while. The next he knew there was a mug in front of him, with warm steam carrying a sweet, slightly sickly odour, and she'd sat opposite him. His hands were still shaking far too much for him to drink. He did manage to speak, though, with an effort. "It wasn't until the last moment I knew he was a man."

He hadn't expected her to understand, and was startled when she replied, "You thought he was a monster."

It was this answer more than her inexplicable kindness that drew Werner back to his senses. He blinked, looked at her properly for the first time, and asked, "Who are you?"

"My name is Frieda," she said. "My husband was Klemens."

"I'm Werner," he replied, and then bowed his head, suddenly afraid. Forgetting her again, he muttered, "What have I done?"

"You've desecrated the body of a good man. Poor boy..."

It took Werner a moment to realise she meant him. He

stared into her eyes, which were as grey as her hair and terrible in the depth of their sadness. He craved suddenly to tell her everything, all that had taken place over the last few months, of the horror that had come to his life and torn it into pieces. But all he said was, "There was a sickness. It came to the animals first, and then to the people. It was like nothing anyone had ever seen – so quick, like a thief in the night. Like something unnatural. It took my father first, and then my mother."

Frieda nodded, and fine wisps of hair fell over her face, so that when she spoke again Werner could barely see her features. "The plague is all across the country, and further as well. It was in the village we left, far to the south. We could do nothing to help, and we feared infection, so we hid ourselves away. My husband's family had lived in that region for centuries. Yet more and more we heard of rumours – they spoke of a monster, and after a time my husband's name was mentioned. Klemens had always had a weak chest. He was very frail. Still, I knew we had to flee."

Werner found it strange to hear this echo of his own life, to see his own ignorance reflected in the prejudice of distant strangers. It had never occurred to him the sickness stretched so far. It had seemed like a curse brought specifically upon them. Then, when a coach thundered from nowhere along the main street, when lights were suddenly seen in the old coast fort, how could these things not be related? Something had come among them, bringing death that fed in the night. It had seemed so clear. "I thought I could make it stop," he whispered hopelessly.

Frieda brushed the hair from her face and regarded him for a long moment. "My husband grew weaker every day. Our servant told me the rumours had followed us, but I knew he couldn't be moved again. We had nowhere else to go, in any case. This morning I sat by his bedside and watched him die. I'm glad you came too late. It would have been terrible for him – and worse for you, perhaps."

"I didn't kill a monster. I didn't save my village."

She looked at him with a curious expression, somehow tender and harsh at once. "Sometimes fate is cruel, and life is hard, and men do awful things. Sometimes the darkness we see is nothing more than a reflection. I must ask for your help before you leave – call it a penance, or a kindness. Will you bury my husband?"

Though Werner couldn't possibly have refused, the deed was nightmarish. As he drew out the stake, as he wrapped the old man in his bed sheets and carried him downstairs, as he dug a hole behind the house, laid his bundle within, and shovelled back the dirt, all he could think of was blood swelling thick between his fingers.

The sky had finally cleared, the rain had stopped, and he realised he'd misjudged the time of day. The sun was only just beginning to break on the horizon when Frieda said goodbye and left him standing beside a fresh grave. He wandered to the front of the house, gazed at the trail that led down to the village. He could see smoke, far below, a single charcoal thread suspended against the glowering orange of the sky. He wanted more than anything to begin down that road, to go home.

Werner looked to his left instead, to where he could just make out the first turn of the coastal highway. He couldn't go back. His deed had severed him forever from the village, as he'd somehow always known it would. He couldn't return. He couldn't save anyone from what was ahead.

The plague would spread, or perhaps disappear of its own accord. Whatever happened, the winter would be fierce and awful and would take more lives.

Nothing he could defeat would redeem those lives.

There was no monster.

~

"A Stare from the Darkness" is perhaps the oldest story in this collection, though it's changed extensively from when it was first written. However its

origin lies, I suspect, in ideas I had left over from when I wrote my MA dissertation, which was theoretically on the subject of C17th Witchcraft but in practise gave me an excuse to go nosing into all sorts of interesting corners, and left me with a fascination with history and folklore that still regularly seeps into my work.

Perhaps needless to point out, "A Stare from the Darkness" was an attempt at deconstructing the traditional vampire myth and examining why such ideas might grow prevalent in the first place. However I also wanted to keep away from any kind of smug, 'gee, weren't people in the past dumb?' kind of narrative, which I suppose was why I tethered the tale so tightly to Werner's perspective.

In the original version, in fact, there was a great deal more of that, and we saw the events that brought Werner to his current pass; this is one of those pieces where the deleted scenes are probably longer in total that the eventual story! It was a tough decision when I finally realised that Werner's entire life history had to go — to be condensed, I think, into all of three lines of dialogue — but in retrospect it was without question the right thing to do.

The Way of the Leaves

What can I do but wait?

I can't go after her – not again. I can't tell the police anything they'll believe. They wouldn't understand. They couldn't.

Who could?

So I sit. I wait. I'm not even sure what for any more. Surely not forgetfulness, because every day I find the past yawning beneath me, a hole I stumble further into. When I resurface, I'm baffled to find myself in the body of a grown man. I wonder who this person is, whose life I've been living. I wonder if anything has felt entirely real since that night.

On my better days, I tell myself that if I can purge these memories there'll be space for something new, that if I hunt hard enough for the past I can halt my slide back into it. Yet another part of me, the greater part, wants to dive into that black lake of memory, maybe for good this time, to submerge and never return.

In the past is a kind of peace, however paper-thin and temporary. In the past is everything I've lost, and everything I once hoped for. Most of all, in the past is Charlotte – and there, at least, I can still reach her.

I could never remember a time when we hadn't been friends.

I won't pretend it was fate, though perhaps – and assuming there's a difference – it could be called inevitable. There was so little to do in the village, and neither of us got on well with other children. We both liked to read, and appreciated solitude. You could say we were forced together, though it never felt like that.

Freedom, even by our limited definition of it, was slow in coming. But eventually we reached an age when the boundaries of the village were no longer absolute. There was only woodland on the three sides away from the main road that eventually led to the motorway. Above the valley, beyond the woods, the crags of the moors stretched away for miles. As long as we kept to the deadlines our parents set for meals and bedtimes they didn't much care if we went walking. We'd wander until we found a spot that held our interest and sit reading, closed in our separate worlds. As we got older and braver, so the destinations became more remote. We took food with us to fend off our return. We came to know the woods, just as well as the old men who still slunk between twilit trees with antique rifles, poaching for rabbits and pheasants.

For all that, it was years before we came across the barrow. It wasn't even far from the village, no more than an hour's walk as the crow flies. But it was hidden well. There was a low hill to the north, which rose up separately from the general incline leading to the moors. We'd always avoided the area because it offered nothing of interest, just a ring of trees at the crest and gorse and brambles making the steep climb difficult on every side.

Finally, having circled the village in every direction and travelled high enough to explore the first purple expanses of heather, we tried the hill just for novelty. It was hard going. We set out early on a Saturday, yet even though we were practised walkers and still close enough to the village to count windows of houses, it was past noon before we neared the top. Our legs and arms were striped with scratches and itched in the late-summer heat. We'd long since abandoned any hopes that the summit would offer something new or interesting, and continued purely through adolescent stubbornness.

The trees circling the top were close-packed, mostly gnarled beech and silver birch, bark peeling like tinfoil.

Bushes had grown to fill the gaps and the soil beneath was barren and dry. There were no gaps, so we crouched to hands and knees and crawled, making our own route as best we could. It seemed to take longer than expected. For what felt like minutes, my perspective was reduced to a lightless canopy of green, the crackle of dry leaves beneath me, the occasional slurred rustling as a breeze soughed through.

When I broke free, I turned straight back to help Charlotte. I remember clearly the expression on her face. She was staring past me, and her eyes gleamed.

"Look," she said.

So I looked.

The summit was small and dark. All of the trees leaned inward, confining the sunlight to a single bright oval above the middle. Just within the outer edge, the ground dipped steeply, forming a kind of natural amphitheatre. A mound rose at the centre, longest on the two edges away from us, almost rectangular, its highest point nearly level with the lowest branches.

"It looks like someone made it."

I nodded. The shape of the mound and the way the bank reached to an even height around it seemed too precise to be accidental.

"Maybe there's a way in," she added.

Without waiting for an answer, Charlotte set off around the circumference. I followed. I was glad our expedition had been rewarded, but I felt anxious as well, though I couldn't explain why. It was cold beneath the trees, cold enough that my flesh goose-pimpled under my thin shirt, yet it was more than that.

When we reached the opposite end, Charlotte pointed. I wondered why at first, since there was just a bush, tangled in a mass like rusted wire. Then I understood. The shadows behind were too black, too deep.

She was right. There was a way in.

Before I could say anything, she'd scrambled down the

embankment and run to the hole.

"There's a sort of arch, with bricks."

When I hurried to stand beside her, I saw that they were more like blocks of stone, pocked and scarred with weathering.

"It looks old," Charlotte said. "But it's too small... too small for a person."

"We could fit," I said, then regretted it so fiercely I bit down on my tongue. Suddenly all I could taste was the warm tang of my own blood.

Charlotte looked at me. "It's too dark."

I nodded, grateful. Yet something in me knew she wouldn't give up so easily.

"We could have a quick look and then come back. We could bring torches."

"There could be..." I trailed off, unable to think of anything so frightening it would deter Charlotte's curiosity. "I'm hungry," I said instead. "We could have lunch and then look, maybe."

"I won't be long."

Charlotte dropped to her knees again and thrust at the bush, trying to clear a way through. It resisted, rustling back into place whenever she moved her hand, snagging on her sleeves and hair. The more she pushed, the more it tangled around her. I didn't try to help, still vaguely hoping she might give up.

Soon, despite the opposition, she'd crawled to a point where her head and shoulders were beyond the stone-rimmed mouth.

"I can see something."

She lay flat and stretched her arms out. Clearly, she still couldn't reach whatever she'd discovered. The darkness seemed to swallow everything beyond the entrance. I could see her shoulders, her upper arms, and then nothing, as if her forearms were simply gone. She struggled forward and abruptly her head was lost too. My stomach tensed, went cold. I wanted to call out, but my jaw seemed too tight.

Suddenly Charlotte was wriggling backwards, I heard her cry, "I've got it," and my stomach unknotted and I could move again. A moment later, she was using one hand to peel the last tendrils of the bush free from her blouse. Her other hand was tightly clenched. Only when she was completely free did she open it and hold her palm up for us both to see. A thin sigh escaped her lips.

"It's beautiful."

It was. But at first I wondered what it could be. While obviously decorative, this wasn't quite like anything I'd ever seen before. Then, as she turned it, I noticed the pin clipped into the back.

"I think it's a brooch," I said. "My mum's got one. Nothing like this, though."

"It must be old."

I understood what she meant. Though the brooch wasn't tarnished, not even dirty, there was a certain crudity to the design. Yet somehow that didn't clash at all with its elegance. It looked as if someone had crafted it, with painstaking care.

"I think it's silver. Is that supposed to be a man?"

"I don't know."

The figure was squat, wide-hipped, with spindly legs that clawed against the brooch's frame just as his hands grasped it to left and right. His features were rough, his hair was shaggy, and from it protruded a pair of goat-like horns that curled to fuse with the ornately decorated border. "Maybe he's a monster... a troll or something."

"Maybe," Charlotte agreed, though with a hint of disappointment in her tone. She curled her fingers and slipped the treasure into a skirt pocket. "Are you still hungry?"

We sat on the bank to eat our sandwiches, neither of us mentioning the mysterious brooch, the hole, or anything else for that matter. When we'd finished, Charlotte drew a book from her satchel and bent over it, reading with her back to me. I followed suit. I sat looking away from the hill, and felt better for doing so.

The book was a new one, by Willard Price I think, luridly covered and easy to lose myself in. I leafed hungrily through the pages. After a while – lying sprawled on the grass and with the sun warm against my face – I found I was reading the same lines over. I closed my eyes, just for a moment.

When I opened them again it wasn't warm any more. I was lying in a lake of shadow, the hiss of wind-rattled leaves in my ears. I rolled over, to see a grey sky thickening with cloud. Where Charlotte had been there was just her satchel. I started, struggled to my feet, and called out.

"What?" Her voice, resentful, came from just beneath me. She'd moved to the bottom of the slope, where the light was better.

"It's getting late."

"I didn't want to wake you."

"I didn't mean to fall asleep. We should get going."

I realised as she stood that she'd been sitting directly in front of the withered bush. I wondered if she'd been reading at all.

Even as we walked around the rim of the outer hill, the clouds seemed to blacken and congeal. It felt as if night was settling, though it could only have been mid-afternoon. The air smelt rain-sodden. We headed for the point where we'd entered, perhaps hoping impractically that the passage we'd made would remain. When we arrived, however, we found the bushes there every bit as impenetrable as elsewhere.

"I'll go first," I said, trying to sound chivalrous.

I crouched and pushed into the undergrowth. This time was even worse. It was pitch-black, and before I was halfway through the rain began, clattering on the branches above. When I struggled into open air, I was almost glad of the heavy drops bursting on my face.

Charlotte let out a sharp cry. I looked back to see her huddled, half-free of the tangling foliage, scrabbling in a pile of tattered birch leaves.

"I dropped it. I've lost it."

"What?"

"The brooch. I dropped it!"

The faded leaves were the colour of slate in the half-light. They came apart in her fingers, crumbling into flakes.

"Couldn't you have lost it before? When you were crawling through?"

"It was here. It was just here."

Her eyes were so full of anger that I knelt to help just to avoid looking at her. When I had no success, I moved to hunt through other similar piles, working outward in a clumsy spiral. But Charlotte never left that spot, just kept turning the same leaves over and over.

Eventually, sounding as if she'd done something terrible, she said, "I lost it."

I abandoned my own half-hearted searching and looked up, to see she was crying. The only time I'd ever seen her cry was when her mother had left the year before.

"We'll come back," I said. "It might be full of things – stuff better than that."

Charlotte looked up. "When?" she asked, in a small voice. "Tonight?"

I hadn't meant it. I just didn't want to watch her crying. "Sure. We'll bring torches. We'll sneak out."

Charlotte nodded, drew a blue-speckled sleeve across her eyes, and suddenly the tears and the helplessness were gone. "My dad's got a good electric torch, and I know where the spare batteries are. I'll make us some more sandwiches, and fill a water bottle. We could bring an axe or something for the bushes."

I felt a shiver, familiar from my time with Charlotte, of excitement edged with fear; partly because of the strange hill and partly the thought of us daring to creep into its black intestine. But what thrilled me more than either was the indistinct sense that it would be the two of us alone in that close darkness.

When I got home, however, the fear began to crystallise. The barrow seemed an abstract menace compared to other very real and mundane dangers.

My parents were liberal enough for people in their time and place, but Charlotte's father was another matter. Though she hardly ever mentioned him, I'd overheard enough of adult conversations to know he was someone to avoid. He spent most nights in the village pub unless they threw him out, as they often did. No wonder his wife had left, they said, when a man behaved like that. Probably he'd done worse things behind closed doors. Why else would a woman flee in the middle of the night, not even taking her own child?

I didn't know how much of this was true, but I knew enough to dread being blamed for something happening to his daughter. I wanted desperately to back out. I teased myself with the possibility, planned how I'd convince Charlotte. I knew all the while that when it came to it I wouldn't. What if she cried again? What if our friendship ended, leaving me alone? And there was more to it than that, of course, far more.

I didn't have much responsibility in our plan, only to show up. Even then, I was late. I'd never crept out in the night before, and more than once, imagined creaks of footsteps froze me in place. Our meeting place was at the south edge of the village, beside the churchyard wall, where the path that led closest to our objective began. Charlotte sat perched on the stile, her black hair almost covering her face, her satchel bulging at her waist. She smiled when she saw me.

We didn't use the torch. One of the decrepit poachers might have been out laying snares, and even in the dark we knew every twist and turn. We didn't speak for a long while, either, not until we were a mile or more from the village.

Then Charlotte whispered, "Thank you."

"For what?"

"For coming."

"I said I would."

She nodded. Then she began to inventory the things she'd brought. She'd been meticulous, so much so that I wondered what she expected to find. Still, it was comforting to imagine we were well-prepared.

The hill wasn't far, and we were more sensibly dressed this time, both in cords and thick cotton shirts. The moon was almost full, and having been up and down once we knew how to avoid the worst patches of gorse and bramble. We earned ourselves fresh scratches, but made quicker progress than in the day.

More than anything, I'd been dreading having to tunnel through the bushes again, this time in darkness. My brain had seized on that, eclipsing any worries about what might happen afterwards. It barely helped when Charlotte volunteered to go first, and I followed so closely that I could have hung onto her boot heel. Yet there was something strangely adventurous about carving through the huddled leaves, encased in the glow of torchlight. Once we broke free, I felt better, braver. I hurried to take the lead.

When I saw the hole, my bravery ebbed away entirely. I thought of a mouth, gaping and eager, and couldn't shake the image. While I stood paralysed, Charlotte kneeled down, pulled a bread knife from her satchel and began to saw at the tendrils blocking our way.

"Are you ready?" she asked, a little breathless.

I shook my head.

"You haven't changed your mind?"

I shook my head again.

"I'll go first," she said. "You can hold the torch."

As she handed it to me, the beam gyrated crazily. Then

she was kneeling again, and crawling against the ravaged bush. I was sure for a moment I'd fail her, that I'd stay with the torch and she'd keep going anyway without me.

That awful idea made me drop to my belly and slither behind her. I was close enough that I didn't realise we were inside the tunnel until Charlotte's foot caught the torch a glancing blow, swerving its beam to illuminate the walls. They arched over us, built of the same stone as the entrance but damp here, stained deep brown in places and patched with moss and lichen.

The space was too narrow to turn around in. Anything could have been behind us, or in front. I'd have frozen again, but instinct insisted it would be worse to be left behind, so I kept moving. My application of the torch was useless, though, and Charlotte must have been moving into utter blackness. If it bothered her, she gave no sign.

I found that I couldn't imagine the world outside, or a sky that wasn't just above my head. All of that seemed unreal. Yet so did the passage, as if it were only a place between places. There was nothing to do but crawl forward, my gaze and every movement bound to Charlotte's shifting outline.

It was when she disappeared that I panicked for real.

A scream caught in my throat and refused to become a sound. It strangled my breathing, throbbed in my chest. I understood with horror and absolute sureness that I was going to suffocate because I was too scared to cry out – and even then, the tumour of noise stayed lodged in my gullet.

Then I heard a sound from ahead, a sigh, and the scream fell out as a long whimper. When I tried to back away, I discovered I'd turned around somehow, and came up hard against the damp stone wall.

"It seems big. I can't see."

"Charlotte?"

"Where are you? I need the torch."

I'd forgotten the torch. Where was it? I realised it had

never left my hand. When I shifted the torch around, the beam streaked up the passage wall – then, just in front of me and above, spilled apart like water. We had reached the end of the tunnel.

I only had to shuffle forward a couple of feet before I could stand up. Charlotte was crouched to one side. I waved the beam around, trying to gauge the dimensions of the space we'd come out in. It wasn't large – the roof was only inches above my head – but was wide enough to make the idea of being inside the inner hill very strange. The ceiling and walls, a single extended arch, were built of the same stones as the entry and passage. I could only stand upright because I was underneath the apex.

Waving the torch close to my feet, I saw more bare stone. I don't know what I'd been expecting; certainly not the treasures I'd promised Charlotte. Yet I was surprised, somehow, to find nothing at all – surprised and relieved. We could leave, now, forget this place. I'd done what I'd said I'd do. Charlotte would get over her disappointment. It would all be over.

"I want to explore," she said.

"There's nothing here."

"There might be something at the other end." Still hunched, she began to move away. "You don't have to come. Shine the torch for me."

I wanted to follow, I did. But my legs were soft as rotten peaches and I could feel the darkness on my back, I could smell it in the dry must of cavernous air. So I stood stock-still and tried to keep the torch on Charlotte, like some old lighthouse keeper struggling to prevent a wreck. All I could do was try and respond to her movements. Even then, they seemed too rapid somehow, as if time itself was playing tricks on me.

"Go slowly," I said, "be careful."

"I *am* being careful."

She looked small and far away. A silhouette, haloed by

light. Every step drew her away from the torch beam.

"Can you hear something?"

I started, felt sweat ice cold beneath my collar.

"No, nothing."

A lie. In the distance, stooped beneath the arched ceiling, she looked like an antique doll. Another swift step drew her entirely into darkness. I swung the beam frantically. I *could* hear something. The air felt thick and close, too heavy to carry proper sound. I didn't cry out. I was scared the air would swallow up the noise.

"I think there's something. There's more, it doesn't end."

The torchlight was dim orange now, as if the dark had clotted around it. Her voice was faint, distorted as by a struggle through water. The other sound was becoming clearer. Like someone singing in a faraway room.

I caught her for a second, an elbow jutting out. Then she slipped free again, and I knew she was gone.

Nearby, very close, someone – something – laughed, with utter contempt.

I barely remember crawling back through the tunnel. I barely remember the mound, the bushes, the trees, or fleeing through tearing thorns towards the path.

Afterwards, in my bedroom, when the shaking had begun to pass and my thoughts were more than the flicker of midsummer lightning, I discovered injuries: scratches, a long cut along my wrist, a scrape of purpling skin beneath the fringe of my hair. I catalogued them with slow care. I didn't think about Charlotte. I dissected each bloody line, every red welt. I didn't think about the darkness or her down in it alone. By the time dawn light began to ease around the curtains I'd inspected every inch of myself, I was only shivering a little, and I was no closer to remembering.

In many ways, that day was the worst. I'd already decided, sitting up in bed amidst sweat-drenched sheets, that

I wouldn't tell. I'd cleaned myself and hidden my dirty clothes before my parents woke. I *couldn't* tell. Charlotte's father, the drunk, the wife-beater, who prowled between home and pub each night, would kill the boy who'd lost his daughter.

The alarm was raised with a 'phone call late in the morning. The first interrogation came from my own father.

"Son, when did you last see Charlotte?"

"Yesterday. Before tea."

"Not after that?"

"Of course not," I said.

If I'd had any skill for dissembling, I'd have dared to sound indignant. I felt like I was exuding guilt through my pores. Only a fool could fail to see it, and my father was no fool.

However, all he did was cough into his fist, stand abruptly and disappear into the living room. I realised I hadn't asked for an explanation, and he certainly hadn't offered one.

Later, after a silent lunch, it was my mother's turn.

"Darling... Charlotte didn't say she was going anywhere? That she was meeting her mother, perhaps?"

"No. Has something happened?"

"She wasn't in bed this morning."

"Oh..." I tried to sound shocked and managed only strangled. "She didn't say anything."

I was horrified with myself, disgusted – I wanted to howl out the truth. But then what? Even if they believed me, even if they could protect me from her father's fury, what could they do? No adult could penetrate that unfathomable blackness. The police would be as helpless as I was.

So the day was passed in listening to my parents debate in other rooms, in rounds of hesitant questioning, 'phone calls back and forth, guilt, fear of being discovered, fear of not being discovered and not knowing which was worse.

After dinner, my parents told me they were going to a

meeting in the church hall.

"Will you go and see your grandma?" my mother asked. "There's some food in the dish with the foil over it. You'd only have to stay a little while."

The reason for my mother's hesitancy was that my grandmother was losing her mind. She spent most of her time lost in a collage of memory, regret and might-have-been. Sometimes she was perfectly lucid, thoughtful and kind and funny. Sometimes she was terrifying, a ghost narrating from some unfathomable netherworld. My mother knew I didn't like to see her and usually honoured our unspoken agreement. Still, I could hardly protest.

"Sure," I said, "I'll go now."

Grandma lived in the next street, just far enough away to preserve her illusion of independence. I knocked on her door, with a porcelain bowl of cottage pie tucked under my arm. I waited a while for an answer and then pushed it open.

"Grandma?"

I pushed on into the kitchen and there she was, sitting at the old pine table amidst a tangle of knitting, red and purple wools spilling riotously to the floor. She smiled when she saw me.

"Mum asked me to bring you some dinner."

"Oh, she's thoughtful. She thinks I can't manage. After all these years, raising her and her two sisters and looking after my Jim, bless him."

"It's just what was left over," I lied.

"Well, she's thoughtful. And you, I haven't see you since... was it Easter? Surely not Christmas?"

I nodded noncommittally. Purely to change the subject I said, "Mum's at a meeting in the church hall."

I regretted it immediately. I wished cruelly that this wasn't a day when my grandmother was alert and full of well-intentioned questions. Yet when she didn't say anything, that turned out to be worse. I had to continue, to fill the vacuum. I told her Charlotte was missing.

"Your friend with the beautiful dark hair? You must be worried out of your wits."

There was something so understanding in her voice. I felt tears throbbing suddenly beneath my eyelids and knew I'd been holding them there by will alone all day. I let out a long sob, and the dam broke.

While my grandmother cradled my head and patted my shoulders, I told her everything. I couldn't help it.

Afterwards, she leaned back in her chair, and her eyes gazing into mine were sharp and glittering as pins. "She's in the barrow? The hill on the hill?"

The barrow? "Yes," I said, "she's down there."

"She's with the Folk then."

I wondered if her mind was wandering again, but her eyes were no less pin-bright. If I didn't know entirely what she meant, it did snag some thread of memory, of stories she'd told me when I was too small to understand.

"The Folk?"

"The Fair Folk. The beautiful people who live beneath the hill."

"I don't understand."

Another lie. For once, my grandmother's words made perfect sense. The old stories were massing in my head like storm clouds: the tales of fairies that were nothing at all like those in any children's book, of conflicts and thefts and uneasy truce. I knew our village had its own long history, had been here since before the Normans came. How much older might that carved-out hill be?

More than that, I knew what I'd seen and heard. That made it easy to believe.

"You'll have to go for her," my grandmother told me, soft and unanswerably strict. "You'll be safer than a grown-up. If they wanted you, they'd have taken you already."

"I'm scared."

"You're right to be. We're stronger than them, though, we're more real. That's why they hide."

She pointed to the doorframe, where a half-dozen tarnished horseshoes hung on a strap of black leather.

"Cold iron. It won't hurt them, not really, but it'll make them think twice about hurting you."

I unhooked the strap. It was good and heavy, long enough to wear around my waist. I felt immediately comforted. "Thank you, Gran."

She smiled sweetly. "Don't thank me. I shouldn't be sending you off like this, but I'm useless, and there's nothing else to do. Be careful. Remember they're not real the way you are."

Then a cloud seemed to pass across her face. She stared away, and looked back unsteadily. When she saw me, it was as if it was for the first time.

"Jim?"

"No Gran."

"Jim," she said, "Where were you last night? It's so cold sometimes. In my feet, it's cold. They told me... I brought flowers, but it rained, and the petals made such a mess."

"Grandma, I have to go."

She nodded. "You'll come back?"

"Sure, Gran, I'll come back."

For a moment, her eyes cleared.

"If a day goes by," she said, "she'll be theirs for good."

I ran home, the horseshoes trailing and clanking behind me. When I saw the house lights were still off, I was grateful and dismayed both at once. There were no excuses any more. It was all real.

I changed back into my already-dirty clothes from the night before and pulled on my thickest coat. I took my dad's torch from the shed and a handful of safety pins from my mother's sewing basket. Carefully, I pinned the belt with its iron weights around my waist and tucked my shirt over it.

Then I ran from the house, fleeing the moment when I'd change my mind and lose even the shred of bravery I had. I kept running as long as I could, hobbled until the stitch in my side let go and ran some more. I jogged up the hill, ignoring thorns and fresh cuts. I plunged through the lightless bushes and burst free on the other side.

My chest was on fire. Now that I had a reason to rush, to numb myself against terror, it was all I could do just to walk. The thought of staying beneath the canopy of trees was too awful to contemplate – branches weaved above, and their shadows lashed the grass around me. The foot of the embankment was too close to the barrow. My only choice was to limp around the rim, my eyes fixed to the wound of moonlight above.

I had no courage left. Even the thought of it seemed hollow. Rounding the corner, seeing the witch-fingered silhouette of the bush, I knew myself perfectly. I'd been too weak to protect Charlotte before. Why should anything be different now?

Yet I didn't dare go home, to tell the truth or try to weave myself deeper into lies. I didn't dare stay where I was. The passage horrified me, but it was somewhere to hide. Creeping past the crooked bush, feeling it try to snare me, was awful. But inside the tunnel, within the torchlight's bright bubble, I felt strangely safe. Perhaps I'd momentarily run out of fear.

Soon the beam found the wider space of the barrow itself and I could stand up. Why had I been so scared? It was just a cave: warm and dry and, to my relief, quite silent. Then I took a step forward and my footstep rang too loud, reverberating from the walls. I shivered but kept moving, shuffling my feet. I held the torch straight out, walking its beam like a tightrope.

My foot struck something soft. A scream choked off in my mouth. It was a body, Charlotte's body, only a few feet from where I'd been. She hadn't disappeared, only fallen and banged her head. No one had laughed. She'd cried out, whimpered for help. And I'd run. I'd abandoned her.

Except that there was no resistance against my foot – a body wouldn't have moved. And I'd have *seen* a body. Breath flooded back into my lungs. I angled the torch down.

Charlotte's rucksack lay half open, her torch beside it. I reached for it with a small sob of relief, put the torch back inside the pack and slung it over my shoulder.

As I stood, I saw something else. I was close to the far end of the barrow, and Charlotte had been right, there was a space: another arch, carved out of the same large blocks as the entrance, only higher and wider. Beyond, a passage curved downward and sharply left. The air was chilled by a slight breeze drifting from below. For a moment, I thought I could hear a hint of rhythm captured in its current.

No. Just my imagination. I stooped under the arch, began to follow the tunnel beyond.

It wasn't long before I felt fear stealing over me again. The passage didn't stop or straighten, and the walls, peculiarly oval, didn't level out. I could only see for a few feet before my view was cut off. The downward slope was steep enough that I had to fight to keep from running.

I realised the tunnel must be twisting like a snail shell down through the hill. If that insight reassured me a little, bringing some rationale to my surroundings, in another way it made the situation infinitely worse. I couldn't help imagining myself descending through the desiccated crust of some vast and ancient crustacean.

I kept walking. I tried to guess at how deep I'd sunk, but it was hopeless. I grew dizzy from always turning. I could have been walking for days, for a thousand miles, sinking corpse-like into the earth.

A sharper bend broke abruptly onto another archway, and beyond the torchlight dissipated and dimmed. I stopped, shuddered, leaned against the wall. There was an awful sense of space. I couldn't see a ceiling or walls, no matter how I twisted the beam.

The air was moist and swam in currents, in and out like

breath. I was conscious of sound again, but as though it had always been there just beneath notice. Though the sound had a musical quality, its tune was alien beyond imagination, a whisper of places I couldn't and shouldn't know.

Over it I heard a cry, a forlorn, incomprehensible ripple of noise.

"Charlotte?"

I barely whispered. I didn't want to be heard. I didn't expect a reply, and none came. I knew it was her.

I stepped into the chamber.

Instantly the sigh of near-music changed, sharpened, and the torchlight sank to a ruddy orange. I felt sure there was something behind me, the same certainty that had peopled my childhood nights with predatory things beneath beds and in wardrobes – but real now, unquestionably real. I heard a flicker of air like wing beats, a delicate hiss. I struggled frantically to tuck my coat inside the belt of horseshoes, so that the metal was exposed. I felt it retreat. I took a step forward, another.

"Charlotte?"

There, in answer, was her outline – just a shade, small and distant. I hurried forward. With every pace, I felt echoes of movements not mine eddying around me. Charlotte didn't look up. She was staring at nothing. I was almost close enough to touch her when she said, "There isn't a door."

"Come on," I replied roughly, and caught hold of her arm.

"Is that you?" She blinked sleepily. "Are you here? I heard her singing."

"We've got to go."

I pulled, and she didn't resist, only looked more confused.

"I waited. I couldn't get in."

I pulled harder. She reeled, and gazed at me in confusion. Her pupils were wide and black in the brassy torch glow.

"*No.*" But when I continued to lead, she didn't fight.

Something brushed my free hand, and I flailed out, almost losing my grip on Charlotte, nearly stumbling. When I looked at my hand, a line of glistening red stretched the length of my palm.

The music quickened, took on a strangled note. I gripped Charlotte's wrist so tightly that my nails broke skin and started to run.

Everything I've described so far seems clear, even now. Beyond that point, it breaks down utterly. I know I ran, pulling Charlotte with me. We fled up the spiral passage, through the barrow, and crawled out of its throat. That's how it must have been. The things I heard, the things I thought I saw – only deep in the worst of sleepless nights do they seem real.

I know for certain we reached the village at a quarter past six in the morning, bruised and exhausted. We were found by the old vicar, Reverend Colgrave, who was up early mowing the grass of the lower churchyard. He says I saw him and called for help, that I was half-carrying Charlotte. I don't remember. He took us into the rectory, laid us both down on his own bed, and called an ambulance, the police and our parents, in that order.

I woke in my own bed. My mother sat beside me. When she saw my eyes open, she gave a little cry and said my name. I tried to sit up, and found that everything hurt. I was in my pyjamas. My hands were bandaged, and there were plasters spaced irregularly up my arms.

"Where's Charlotte?"

It seemed strange to me that we'd been separated.

"She's in the hospital. She's been sleeping too. The doctors say she's had a knock on the head, but they're sure she'll wake up soon."

I nodded, not realising what she meant. She offered me

a glass of water and I emptied it in one long gulp.

"I'm going to get your father now. He's been worried. We've both been very worried." She looked for a moment as if she'd begin to cry. "He might ask you some questions. If you're not ready to talk, he'll understand."

There *were* questions, inevitably, from my father and later from the police. There were some answers as well, though they didn't come from me. I knew instinctively that telling the truth was impossible. I arrived, instead, at a compromise. I'd gone out to look for Charlotte at a spot I knew she liked. When I'd found her, something awful had happened, something so terrifying I couldn't talk about it. When pressed, I claimed not to remember. It seemed sensible. In the books I liked, the characters were often struck with amnesia under dramatic circumstances.

It didn't really matter whether anyone believed me. There was no way to prove my obstinacy was due to anything other than a blank patch in my mind.

Fortunately, and to my complete surprise, the greatest holes in my story were taken care of by Reverend Colgrave. The first Sunday after church, he suggested to my parents that perhaps a private discussion of our last meeting might jog my memory. Once we were alone, he presented me with the belt of horseshoes.

"Where did you get this? What on Earth did you want it for?"

"I don't know."

He sighed bitterly. "I think I do. There are people in this village who say stupid, blasphemous things. I took this from you because I won't have those superstitions encouraged. I suspect you've listened to them, and that's why your friend is lying in a hospital bed now. I only hope you've learned your lesson."

I nodded. What would have been the point in telling him that listening to my grandma had likely saved Charlotte's life?

"I'll never do it again," I said, vague but truthful.

Reverend Colgrave had, for his own reasons, covered up most of the physical evidence of that night.

There was no one else who could contradict my version of events. As my mother had tried to tell me that first morning, Charlotte was comatose and had been since our return. There was no head wound, my mother had invented that particular detail. The doctors had discovered no real damage, in fact, beyond scratches, dehydration and bruises. They'd put her unconsciousness down to shock rather than injury.

She woke on the fifth night.

Her story, as it turned out, was much like mine. She really didn't remember anything of our trips to the barrow. She spent time with a psychiatrist as part of the police investigation, trying to patch together the broken web of her memory. It was hopeless. With no proof of a crime, no proof of anything, they eventually gave up. In the absence of facts, rumour spread. Though I only realised it years later, there were those in the village who thought I'd raped Charlotte; that she kept quiet from fear. Others accused her father, though never to his face.

All I knew was that we were kept apart. Gradually, though, with the passage of months, the cordon began to crumble. My parents relented, unsure of what they were punishing me for, and Charlotte's father hadn't enough control over his own life, let alone hers, to impede us.

When I saw her, finally, we didn't talk about what had happened. I wouldn't have, even if I'd thought Charlotte remembered. The barrow had fired my nightmares for long months and I had no desire to stir the embers. Nor did I feel that our friendship had been damaged – only interrupted.

Still, the months apart had changed things. We weren't children any longer, and the things I'd begun to notice about Charlotte were increasingly hard to ignore. She was beautiful, even then, in a serene and almost melancholy way that hypnotised me. I didn't so much as fall in love as realise I'd loved her all along.

The year I turned eighteen my grandmother – long since lost in senility – died a quiet death in a rest home some miles from the village. She left me her house in her will. I'd just started my first proper job, as an apprentice librarian in the nearest town. Suddenly, it seemed I was an adult, complete with property and prospects.

I asked Charlotte if she'd marry me, and she said yes.

Life was almost perfect. Everything was as it should be, as it always should have been.

I was lying to myself, of course. I think I always knew that. There were signs, and I wasn't blind. Perhaps I pretended they didn't matter. If I did, I was wrong, and cruel as well. Charlotte was unhappy and I said nothing, did nothing.

No, that's not true. I did the things men do to try to make their wives happy. I loved her absolutely and showed it in every way I could. But I understood deep down that it would never work. What made Charlotte sob in her sleep, what overcast her face, was older and deeper than anything as simple as our marriage.

Steadily, things worsened. Charlotte sank into black moods. I'd come home to find her pacing back and forth, head tilted, as if listening to noises only she heard. I was woken often, in the stretch between midnight and dawn, by her talking in her sleep. I couldn't understand the words she mumbled. Eventually I realised why: whatever language she was speaking, it wasn't English.

As the years passed, so our marriage deteriorated, from apparent perfection to terrible masquerade. The more I realised the inside was broken, the more I struggled to preserve the façade. I lost my temper, accusing her wildly, shouting when I came home to find her absorbed in privacy

I couldn't touch. Slowly, by degrees, I grew cruel.

Charlotte first disappeared ten years after our wedding. I woke to blackness, rolled over, wondered for a moment at the cold – and realised I was alone. I didn't stop to dress. I threw on a dressing gown and shoes, and hurried into the darkness. I knew without thinking where I was going.

Sure enough, I found her on the edge of the village, approaching the stile with slow, shuffling steps. She didn't respond when I called her name. I realised she was asleep, though her eyes were just barely open. I led her home, eased her into an armchair and wrapped a blanket round her. Finally, she blinked and looked up at me.

For once, I didn't shout. Some instinct told me we were beyond the point where it could serve any purpose. Instead, I knelt, took her hands and said, "I love you. Don't you love me?"

"Of course I do."

"Then why?"

She shook her head. She knew as well as I did that there was no answer. We cried, and held each other. Later we made love, for the first time in weeks.

I knew through every moment that I'd lost her.

Three more times she went out into the night, three more times I brought her back. On the fourth, I woke with an awful sense of emptiness in my stomach. I pulled on my clothes and ran to the barrow, up the old trail, up the hillside, through the matted foliage at its crest. She wasn't there. A scrap of white cloth hung on the gnarled bush at the entrance, like a minute flag of surrender. I recognised it as part of her nightgown.

I vaguely remember walking home. I remember sitting, not capable of thinking, watching the light change in the window. The 'phone rang, and I picked it up because it was beside my hand. I didn't say anything. I could hear my mother's voice calling my name. I heard an edge of worry creep into it, followed by the beginnings of panic.

"Are you there? Are you sick? Has something happened?"

"Charlotte's gone."

"What? Gone where?"

"Gone. She's gone."

"Have you done anything? Have you called the police?"

"No."

"You should call the police."

So I did.

Once again, I found myself unable to tell the truth. This time it was harder, because the half-truths were worse. The police formed a picture of a husband who tormented his wife until she fled in despair and I was helpless to alter it. I doubted they would have helped even if they could have. How much effort would they expend in bringing a desperate woman back to her bullying husband?

I didn't entirely blame them.

Three days after Charlotte's disappearance there was a knock on the door. I assumed it was the police again, and steeled myself for more questions. When instead I recognised Charlotte's father there on the doorstep, I stood speechless. I'd hardly seen him in all the time we'd been married.

"There's something I need to tell you," he said.

He'd obviously been drinking, the air reeked of whisky; but after all those years, he must have been almost inured to it.

"Come in."

I led him into the living room, pointed out a chair. He glanced at it and stayed standing in the doorway. I don't know what I was expecting. The old childish fear of him hovered close to the surface of my mind.

"I know it all," he said, and then, "It's not your fault."

"I don't understand." I thought it was the alcohol talking, of course.

"Everyone blamed me... I've lived with that. Now it's your turn. There's no way round it. I could have told you, but what would have been the point? I hoped it might be different. And if it wasn't, you couldn't have changed things."

"Will you sit down? I don't know what you're talking about."

He sighed, leaned back against the doorframe.

"She left, and it wasn't my fault, just like this isn't yours. Charlotte's mother left to be with her own kind. Now Charlotte has too. If anyone's to blame, it was her mother and me. I shouldn't have fallen in love with her. We should never have had a child. She was just a creature that didn't like its life and tried another, to see how it fit."

He took a step back, and anger flared in his eyes.

"You should be glad ... at least Charlotte *tried* to stay with you."

He turned and marched from the room. I heard the front door slam.

I thought about going after him, about all the questions I wanted answers to. But I knew, deep down, that he'd given me all the answers I really needed.

It makes sense, as much as anything can.

I remember the rumours about Charlotte's parents: how her mother appeared from nowhere and before anyone knew, they were married; how everyone assumed she'd eloped from one of the nearby villages. I suppose they were right, in a way – they just underestimated how far she'd come. When she disappeared, the gossips thought she'd regretted her rash choice and gone back home. Again, perhaps they weren't far from the truth.

The only thing I wonder is whether she left her daughter behind from kindness or cruelty – or some altogether different motive I can't begin to understand. Maybe, from the beginning, we were caught in something vaster and more complicated than we could have imagined. Maybe our love was mired in centuries-old politics, or circumstances grander and older than politics that I have no word for. Maybe we never stood a chance.

Maybe all I'm doing is hunting for excuses.

I'd ask Charlotte's father, but something in me knows he's told me all he has to say. Anyway, I wouldn't make him tear open old wounds again. I know what it's like to live every moment in fear of the past. I know the weight of a loss you can never entirely understand.

And I won't be ungrateful. He gave me some comfort. I understand how hard Charlotte must have tried to be with me. She fought. She stayed against her instincts. That has to count for something.

The least I can do in return is wait.

The least I can do is believe she might come home.

~

I've never been one for following that old chestnut about writing what you know, but of all the stories in this collection, barring "The Untold Ghost", "The Way of the Leaves" comes closest. Which is a strange thing to say on the face of it because, when I stop to consider, there isn't a single detail anywhere that's even close to my own childhood. But I remember thinking while I was writing this one about my grandmother, the Yorkshire village where she lives and the hill nearby, even if the end result reflects none of those things in any recognisable way.

Still, whenever I come back to "The Way of the Leaves" I feel an odd sense of familiarity. The only explanation I can come up with is that, when I was the age the protagonists start out as, this is something like the fantastical version of my childhood I might have imagined for myself: a countryside setting, secret passages, hidden caves, and a Willard Price reference to boot. It's certainly a nostalgic story, even if it also happens to be about the perils of nostalgia. Like a lot of the tales in this book, it turns in on itself before the end and begins to undermine its own assumptions. Resurrecting the past becomes in itself a dangerous act, one that can ultimately lead only to grief and self-delusion.

On a side note, it's fair to say that this collection would never have happened were it not for "The Way of the Leaves", which won the first (and

*indeed last) Spectral Press chapbook competition, and first gave me the idea
that it might be pretty cool to have all of these classically-styled horror and
dark fantasy tales together in the one place.*

Slow Drowning

Had there been a noise? Like chattering, low, small voices?

Marjorie rolled over, groped instinctively for the warm body beside her – and recoiled as if stung from its absence.

She forced her eyes open to stare at the clock, waited for the figures to focus: they read 03:52. As she slithered from beneath the quilt, Marjorie wondered distantly how anyone could stay sane on so little sleep.

Peter had always slept badly. He had turned and turned, and most nights he'd woken her. Then she'd snap, call him selfish and worse, and he'd slip out of bed and disappear downstairs. She'd never thought to ask what he did in those hours of banishment.

At the memory, something caught in her throat. She ran a sleeve across her eyes, and held her breath.

The something retreated.

In the kitchen, she began to prepare Horlicks. Then, remembering she wouldn't be capable of sleep again for hours, she emptied the mulch into the sink and fished for the coffee instead.

When sitting made her cramped, she took to pacing instead, navigating the kitchen like a swimmer making laps. On her third turn she strayed too close to the patio doors and the outside light strobed on. It stung her aching eyes, but did nothing to illuminate the garden, served only to force it into deeper blackness. She turned the key in the door and slid it open.

Outside, bathed in astringent light, she felt exposed in her thin dressing gown – as though she were being watched, condemned. But the eyes of neighbouring windows were curtained, and there was no one to see.

There was no one to see but *them*.

She hissed between her teeth, remembering the whispers that had woken her. She hadn't dared to come out here, not since that day – hadn't dared to face them, or him. She hadn't meant to be here now. Yet she could hear the slap of her soles on the damp flagstone path. There was no avoiding it, it seemed.

Still, when she drew near the pond she stopped short and hugged the mug to her breast, seeking comfort in its warmth. The surface of the water was still and black. Did fish sleep? Were they lurking blank-eyed beneath the surface, dreaming of other, greater waters?

She hadn't seen his body, not properly; just an outline, face down. She remembered screaming. Perhaps she'd cried his name. Inside, she couldn't find the phone, though it was in its cradle as always. She didn't remember calling the police, or opening the door, or leading them to the garden.

Her memories picked up with them all sitting on plastic patio chairs. There was a blanket round her shoulders, and she was pretending to drink tea that had materialised from somewhere. One of them was asking her questions. Did he drink? Was he taking any medication? Why would he have been outside so late at night? Marjorie didn't know. Only then had she realised how much of Peter's life was a mystery to her.

The days after were a blur. Friends visited, tried futilely to hold lopsided conversations. Then there had been a call that wasn't a well-wisher, something she couldn't ignore. Minutes later, she was sitting again with the young policewoman, trying to listen to terrible, impossible statements:

"Almost a bottle of whisky,"... "Think he tripped, banged his head,"... "Not treating it as suspicious or intentional."

"Intentional?"

"As a suicide."

There was a bench beside the pond. Peter had made it over the course of a week's leave. It creaked dangerously as Marjorie lowered herself onto it.

From the other side of the pond, eight eyes stared blankly back. She assumed they were supposed to look charming, in their flamboyant coats and off-kilter hats. The one on the left carried a fishing rod that drooped towards the ebony water. His partner was driving a shovel towards the ground. Another was waving, and the fourth rested his chin on his fist as though deep in thought.

Peter had tried to tell her their names once, and she'd reminded him how ridiculous it was, no better than playing with dolls. This garden had been his escape from her – even before his final escape, his pitiful drunken exit from her life.

"It was you," she addressed them. "You took him away."

Day by day, he'd drifted out here, away from her and into endless projects. There was always a wall to construct, a flowerbed to arrange. As the garden had become more his, so she'd dared less and less to follow him.

Wasn't that why she'd been cruel? If she had been, that was the reason. For love. For what could have been. She'd always known there was some perfect isolation that would plaster over every fracture. When he'd stopped seeing the last of his friends, she'd thought that would be it.

The garden had been a wilderness then. She'd never imagined it could be an escape route.

"He was supposed to be mine and you took him away."

Marjorie stood, walked round the edge of the pond. She picked up the first gnome, the one with the fishing rod, and held it up. Its eyes were crude black circles, its mouth a ragged line. She hurled the figure onto the slime-edged stones and watched with satisfaction as it shattered messily.

The second she threw with all her strength towards the patio. She didn't see its demise, but heard it explode against the flagstones.

The third she used as a club to assault the fourth, and when its head came off and spun away into the grass, tossed into the pond and kicked its companion after.

Then she walked back round to retrieve her coffee, and was pleased to find it still warm. She took a last sip, poured the remainder into the pond.

It would only keep her awake. And she didn't think she'd have any more trouble sleeping.

~

One of two short stories I've written involving garden gnomes; in this one they get horribly mutilated and in the other they declare war against all of humanity, which suggests I have a much bigger problem with gnomes than I've ever suspected. This started out as a more serious tale, but the moment those pesky ornaments showed up a note of black comedy began to intrude!

About The Author & Artist

David Tallerman is the author of the comic fantasy novels *Giant Thief*, *Crown Thief* and *Prince Thief*, the absurdist steampunk graphic novel *Endangered Weapon B: Mechanimal Science*, and the Tor.com novella *Patchwerk*.

His short fantasy, science fiction, horror and crime stories have appeared in around eighty markets, including *Clarkesworld*, *Nightmare*, *Alfred Hitchcock's Mystery Magazine* and *Beneath Ceaseless Skies*.

David can be found online at davidtallerman.co.uk.

Duncan Kay is an artist and designer living in Glasgow. His work can be found online at:
https://www.artstation.com/artist/duncankayart